"Then why did you come here today?"

He smiled, and she knew she would remember the chill of that smile forever.

"I came to tell you what happens next," he said softly.

"What—what happens next?"

Cullen nodded. He'd thought about this a thousand times…. Like it or not, the child growing in Marissa Perez's womb was his. Like it or not, he was responsible not just for its conception but for its life. Like it or not, by late last night he could think of only one appropriate plan of action.

"What happens next," he said slowly, his eyes on Marissa's face, "is that you're going to become my wife."

Dear Reader,

Welcome to the exciting world of the O'Connells. Keir, Cullen and Sean are sexy, exciting men. Their sisters, Fallon, Megan and Brianna, are strong, independent women. What do they all have in common? They're all going to risk everything to find everlasting love.

Claiming His Love-Child is Cullen's story. He's a handsome, successful bachelor. He's watched Keir find a woman and fall head over heels in love. He's just seen Fallon marry the man of her dreams. But would *he* ever trade his freedom for a wedding ring? No way, Cullen says…but life has a way of surprising us.

After a night of searing passion, Cullen O'Connell can't forget Marissa. But when the top lawyer tracks her down, he's in for a shock…she's pregnant! If Cullen wants to claim his love-child, he reckons there's only one thing to do—offer Marissa marriage. But will she accept?

I think their story will grab you by the heart. That's what it did to me as I wrote it.

With love,

Sandra Marton

Look for the next exciting installment of the
O'Connell saga

The Sheikh's Convenient Bride
#2410
Coming August 2004

Sandra Marton

CLAIMING HIS LOVE-CHILD

The O'CONNELLS

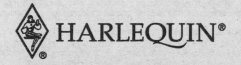

HARLEQUIN®

TORONTO • NEW YORK • LONDON
AMSTERDAM • PARIS • SYDNEY • HAMBURG
STOCKHOLM • ATHENS • TOKYO • MILAN • MADRID
PRAGUE • WARSAW • BUDAPEST • AUCKLAND

ISBN 0-373-12387-6

CLAIMING HIS LOVE-CHILD

First North American Publication 2004.

This edition published by arrangement with Harlequin Books S.A.

® and TM are trademarks of the publisher. Trademarks indicated with ® are registered in the United States Patent and Trademark Office, the Canadian Trade Marks Office and in other countries.

Visit us at www.eHarlequin.com

Printed in U.S.A.

CHAPTER ONE

July, the coast of Sicily

MEMORIES of the woman and the long, hot night she'd spent in his arms were demons that haunted Cullen O'Connell's waking and sleeping hours.

He didn't like it. What was she doing in his head? The sex had been great. Okay, incredible, but sex was all it was. She was bright and beautiful, but he hardly knew her. Outside the context of the night they'd spent together, she meant nothing to him.

Cullen had no reason to think about her, especially now.

He was in Italy to celebrate his sister's marriage with the rest of his family. The past few days had been great. Whether they were partying or just sitting around talking, Cullen had never found better company than his brothers. Add his three sisters to the mix, things only got better. Toss in his mother and stepfather for good measure, you had a gathering of the O'Connell clan that would put any other party to shame.

As for the setting—most people would call it idyllic. *Castello* Lucchesi stood on a cliff overlooking the Mediterranean with Mount Etna, trailing ribbons of fire, as a backdrop.

The perfect setting for the perfect party. Cullen's mouth thinned. Then, why was he so restless? Why was he thinking about a woman he barely knew? Why this increasing desire to head home to Boston?

Too much togetherness?

Maybe.

Cullen sighed, undid the jet studs at the collar and cuffs of his frilled white shirt, rolled the sleeves back on his tanned, muscled forearms and stared out over the sea. He'd already discarded the jacket of his tux, left it draped over one of the little white folding chairs in the garden of the *castello*.

It had never happened before. Well, there was a first time for everything.

Maybe it was the occasion making him feel edgy. This was the third O'Connell wedding in two years. First his mother's, then his brother Keir's, and now his sister Fallon had tied the knot.

Or the noose, Cullen thought as he went up the winding steps that led to the crenellated watchtower overlooking the castle and the Mediterranean.

What was it about weddings that made women weep and men want to run for the hills?

At least this one had been unusual. The high cliff, the blue sea, the magnificent castle…

Cullen smiled.

And that game of touch football yesterday, on the beach below the castle. The Shirts—Megan, Briana and Fallon—had come within one touchdown of trouncing the skins—Sean and Cullen, with Keir and Fallon's groom, Stefano, spelling each other.

Meg had protested. "No fair. That's four to three."

"It isn't," Cullen had insisted. "The four of us don't play at the same time. And you're a fine one to talk about what's fair, considering that you darned near fractured three of my ribs with that elbow of yours."

"Yeah," Bree said, poking out her chin, "but that only means you've always got a fresh player with unbroken ribs on the field."

"Well, you've got a cheering section building your morale," Cullen had retaliated.

They'd all looked at Keir's pregnant wife, Cassie, sitting

on the sidelines. Cassie had grinned, pumped both fists in the air and yelled, *Yea,* which was exactly the distraction Meg needed to shout "Fumble," scoop up the ball and charge across the goal line.

"Cheater!" Cullen had yelled, and his sisters said, yeah, right, and so what? All was fair in love, war and football.

Somehow they'd all ended up in the pool, laughing and ducking each other under the water. Well, all except Stefano and Fallon, who'd wandered off alone, gazing into each other's eyes. And Keir and Cassie had stayed on the sidelines, too, with Keir hovering over his wife as if she were made of crystal.

Cullen leaned out of the tower's embrasure, which still bore the warmth of the sun that was only now starting to lower in the sky.

The last few days had been fun. The evenings, too. Lots of good food and *vino,* and plenty of time for Stefano to get to know them and them to get to know him. It had all been great…except for those unwanted flashes of memory. The X-rated images, captured forever in his head.

Marissa, whispering his name. Clinging to him. Moving beneath him, taking him deep, so deep, inside her…

"Hell," Cullen muttered. It was pretty sad when a grown man could turn himself on by thinking back to something that had happened two months ago.

Exhaustion could explain it. He'd flown in Friday, straight from a week of twelve-hour days spent between his office and the courtroom. Combine that with jet lag, a Sicilian heat so oppressive you could almost feel it melting your bones, toss in worry about Fallon's accident and the scars left on her lovely face, and he had every right to be a basket case.

At least he wasn't worried about Fallon anymore. His sister was so happy, so beautiful, so cherished by her new husband that it was a joy to see.

As for all this stuff about a woman he hardly knew… There was no point in trying to figure it out. What he needed was a breather. A real one. A true break in routine. The case back home was done with; he had nothing urgent on his agenda. He could change his flight, go to Nantucket instead of Boston, provision his boat, take her out to sea for a few days. Or fly to his cabin in Vail. The Rockies were spectacular in the summer; he'd always meant to do some hiking but he hadn't found the time. Well, he'd find it now, pick up some stuff and backpack.

Or he could go to Madrid. Or London. He hadn't been there in a while. He could go to Maui, or the Virgin Islands.

He could go to Berkeley.

Cullen blinked. Berkeley, California? His alma mater, the place where he'd taken his law degree? It was an okay place but it wasn't exactly one of the world's premier vacation spots.

Yes, but Marissa Perez was there.

Back to square one. Man, he definitely needed a change! Sure, she was in Berkeley. So what? He'd spent a couple of evenings with her. Okay. A weekend.

And he'd spent one night, or most of it, with her in his bed.

Maybe the best thing was to let the images come instead of fighting them. Lessen their impact by letting them wash over him, like a wave hitting the beach far below the tower.

Simply put, Marissa Perez had been spectacular in the sack.

He'd never had a better time in bed, and that was saying a lot. Only a foolish man lied to himself and Cullen had never been a fool. It was simple honesty to admit he was a man who had a knack for getting it on with the opposite sex. Truth was, that knack had brought him more than his fair share of women who were beautiful and exciting and bright and great between the sheets.

For all of that, he'd never enjoyed sex with any of them as much as he had with Marissa.

Cullen scowled and turned his back to the sea.

Out of bed had been another story.

Oh, the lady was beautiful. Exciting. And bright. But she was as prickly as the cactus plants that grew on the sides of these Sicilian roads, as sullen as Mount Etna looming over the sea. She made him uncomfortable, for God's sake, and why would a man put up with a woman who did that?

Hold a door open for her, she gave you a look that said she was perfectly capable of opening it herself. Start to pull out her chair at a restaurant, she grabbed it first. Try to talk to her about anything but the law and the topic you were going to present over Alumni Weekend and she took you straight back to it, reminded you, though politely, that she was here only because she'd been chosen to be your liaison during your couple of days on campus.

Cullen's mouth hardened.

The lady had an attitude. She'd done her best to make it clear dealing with him was a chore she hadn't wanted but despite or maybe because of it, there'd been an almost instantaneous flash of heat between them, right from the minute she picked him up at the airport. Then, on Saturday night, she'd been making some stiff little good-night speech in the car outside his hotel when all at once the rush of words had stopped, she'd looked at him and he'd reached for her…

And changed things by taking her to bed.

No more haughty intellectual talk about torts and precedents. No more stiff insistence on proving her independence. Not during that long, hot night together. She'd said other words, instead, gone pliant in his arms, uttered soft cries of pleasure as he touched her, tasted her, filled her…

"Got to tell you, bro, a man looks like that, his thoughts are probably X-rated."

Cullen looked down. Sean was climbing the watchtower steps. He took a deep breath, forced those last images from his mind and smiled at his kid brother.

"Pathetic," he said lazily, "that all you can think of is sex."

"The point is, what were *you* thinking of, Cull? From the expression on your face, she must be amazing."

"She is," Cullen said, deadpan. "I was admiring the volcano."

"Etna?" Sean nodded. "Quite a lady, all right, but I'm not buying it. Only a geologist would get that glint in his eye over a volcano."

"Vulcanologist, and is that why you came up here? To take notes on the volcano?"

"I came to escape our sisters. Meg and Bree are back to sobbing into their handkerchiefs, and now Ma and Cassie have joined in."

"Well," Cullen said, grinning, "what do you expect? They're women."

"I'll drink to that."

"So would I, but it would mean we'd have to go back to the terrace."

"No, it wouldn't."

Sean winked and pulled a pair of sweating green bottles from his rear trouser pockets. Cullen clapped a hand to his heart.

"No," he said dramatically. "It can't be!"

"It can."

"Beer? Honest-to-God beer?"

"Better. Ale. Irish ale. Here. Take yours before I change my mind and drink them both."

Cullen took the bottle Sean held out. "I take back everything I ever said about you. Well, maybe not everything, but a man who can find Irish ale at a Sicilian wedding can't be all bad."

The brothers smiled at each other and took long, satisfying drinks of the cold ale. After a minute, Sean cleared his throat.

"Anything on your mind? Anything you want to talk about, I mean? You've been kind of quiet."

Cullen looked at his brother. *Yes,* he thought. *I want to talk about why in hell I should still be thinking about a woman I slept with one time, weeks and weeks ago...*

"You bet," he said, with a quick smile. "Let's talk about how you snagged this ale, and what it'll take to get us two more bottles."

Sean laughed, as Cullen had hoped he would. The conversation turned to other things, like how weird it was to see Keir hovering over his pregnant wife.

"Who'd have believed it?" Sean said. "Big brother, talking about babies... Is that what happens when a man marries? He turns into somebody else?"

"*If* he marries, you mean. Hell, how'd we end up on such a depressing topic? Marriage. Children." Cullen shuddered. "Let's go see about the ale," he said, and just that easily, Marissa Perez went back to being nothing more important than a memory.

HOURS later, in a jet halfway over the Atlantic, Cullen looked at the flight attendant hovering over him in the darkened comfort of the first-class cabin.

"No coffee for me, thanks," he told her.

"No supper? No dessert? Would you like something else, Mr. O'Connell?"

Cullen shook his head. "I spent the weekend at a wedding in Sicily."

The flight attendant grinned. "Ah. That explains it. How about some ice water?"

"That would be perfect."

Truth was, he didn't want the water, either, but she meant well and he had the feeling saying "yes" to something was the only way he'd convince her to leave him alone. She brought the glass, he took a perfunctory sip, then put it aside, switched off the overhead light, put his seat all the way back and closed his eyes.

Whatever had been bothering him had faded away. Talking to Sean had done it, or maybe all that goofing around in the garden. Everyone except Keir and Cassie, their mother and stepfather had ended up in the pool again. Well, Stefano and Fallon hadn't been there, either, but nobody had expected them to be. After that, they'd all changed to dry clothes, the mood had mellowed and they'd sat around in the encroaching darkness, talking quietly, reminiscing about the past.

One by one, the O'Connells had finally drifted off to bed. All but Cullen, who, it turned out, was the only one of them who'd made arrangements to fly home that night instead of the next day.

On the way to the airport, he'd thought about the ideas that had floated through his mind earlier. Going to Nantucket instead of straight home, or to Colorado, or someplace in Europe...

Why would he do that?

Whatever had been bugging him was long gone. He'd climbed out of the back seat of Stefano's limousine feeling relaxed and lazy, gone to the first-class check-in line, had time for a coffee prior to boarding.

He still felt relaxed. He liked flying at night. The black sky outside the cabin, the gray shadows inside, the sense that you were in a cocoon halfway between the stars and the earth.

That was how he'd felt that night after he'd taken Marissa to bed. Holding her in his arms, feeling her warm and soft against him until she'd suddenly stiffened, started to pull away.

"I have to go," she'd said, but he'd drawn her close again, kissed her, touched her until she moaned his name and then he'd been moving above her, inside her, holding back, not letting go because she wasn't letting go, because he had the feeling she'd never flown free before and the first time it happened, it was damn well going to be with him...

"Damn," he said softly.

Cullen's eyes flew open. He put his seat up, folded his arms and glowered into the darkness.

So much for feeling nice and relaxed.

This was stupid. Worse than stupid. It was senseless. Why was Marissa in his head? He hadn't seen her since that night. She'd left his bed while he was sleeping, hadn't shown up to take him to the airport, hadn't answered her phone when he called. Not that morning, not any of the times he'd tried to reach her after he was home again.

He always got her answering machine.

You've reached Marissa Perez. Please leave a brief message and I'll get back to you as soon as possible.

His last message had been brief, all right, even curt.

"It's Cullen O'Connell," he'd said. "You want to talk to me, you have my number."

She'd hadn't phoned. Not once. Her silence spoke for itself. They'd slept together, it had been fun, and that was that. No return visits, no instant replays. End of story.

Fine with him. The trouble with most women was that you couldn't get rid of them even after you explained, politely, that it was over.

Cullen? It's Amy. I know what you said, but I was thinking…

Cullen? It's Jill. About what we decided the other night…

Marissa Perez took an admirable approach to sex. A man's approach. She took what she wanted and shut the door on what she didn't. That didn't bother him. It didn't bother him at all.

Why would it?

For all he gave a damn, she could have slept with a dozen men since that night with him. After all, he'd had several women in his life since that weekend. Okay, he hadn't taken any of them to bed, but so what? He'd been working his tail off. Besides, a short break from sex was a good thing. It only heightened the pleasure in the future.

Tomorrow, he'd phone the blonde he'd met at that cocktail party last week. Or the attorney from Dunham and

Busch with the red hair and the big smile. She'd come on to him like crazy.

Definitely, he'd celebrate his homecoming with a woman who'd be happy to take his calls and happy to see him. And he'd sleep with her, make love until crazy thoughts about Marissa Perez were purged from his mind. Surely, his memories of that night were skewed.

Cullen muttered a couple of raw words under his breath as he sat up and switched on his overhead light. To hell with what time it was in New York. The blonde from last week was a party animal. This hour of the night, she was probably just coming in the door.

He dug his address book and his cell phone from his pocket, tapped in her number. She answered after two rings, her voice husky with sleep.

"H'lo," she said. "Whoever you are, you'd better be somebody I really want to talk to."

He smiled, turned his face to the window and the night sky. "It's Cullen O'Connell. We met last—"

"Cullen." The sleep-roughened voice took on a purr. "I'd started to think you weren't going to phone."

"I had things to clear up. You know how it is."

"No," she said, and gave a soft laugh, "I don't know how it is. I guess you'll just have to show me."

Cullen felt the tension drain away. "My pleasure," he said, imagining her as she must look right then, sleep-tousled and sexy. "How about tonight? I'll pick you up at eight."

"I already have a date for tonight."

"Break it."

She laughed again and this time the sound was so full of promise that he felt a heaviness in his groin.

"Are you always this sure of yourself?"

He thought of Marissa, of how she'd slipped from his bed, how she'd ignored his phone calls…

"Eight o'clock," he repeated.

"You're an arrogant SOB, Mr. O'Connell. Luckily for you, that's a trait I like in a man."

"Eight," Cullen said, and disconnected.

He put away his cell phone, sat back and thought about the evening ahead. Dinner at that French place. Drinks and dancing at the new club in SoHo. And then he'd take the blonde home, take her to bed, and exorcise the ghost of Marissa Perez forever.

CHAPTER TWO

September: Boston, Massachusetts

THE end of summer always came faster than seemed possible.

One minute the city was sweltering in the heat and the Red Sox were packing in the ever-faithful at Fenway Park. Next thing you knew, gray snow was piled on the curbs, the World Series was only a memory and the Sox hadn't even made it to the playoffs.

Cullen stepped out of the shower, toweled off and pulled on a pair of old denim shorts.

Not that any of that had happened yet.

It was Labor Day weekend, the unofficial end of summer with the real start of fall still almost three weeks away. Cold weather was in the future, and so was the possibility, however remote, that Boston could rise from the ashes and at least win the division championship.

Cullen strolled into the kitchen and turned on the TV in time to catch the tail end of the local news. The Sox had lost a tight game yesterday; nobody had much hope they'd do any better today, said the dour-faced sportscaster.

"Wonderful," Cullen muttered as he opened the refrigerator, took out a bottle of water and uncapped it.

The sports guy gave way to the weatherman. Hot and humid, the weatherman said, with his usual in-your-face good cheer. Saturday, 10:00 a.m. and the sun was blazing from a cloudless sky, the temperature was pushing ninety with no break in sight from now through Monday.

"A perfect holiday weekend," the weather guru said as if he'd personally arranged it.

Cullen scowled and hit the off button on the remote.

"What's so perfect about it?" he growled. It was just another weekend, longer than most, hotter than most. Long, hot, and...

And, what was he doing here?

Nobody, but nobody, stayed in town Labor Day weekend. Driving home from his office yesterday, traffic going out of the city had been bumper to bumper. He'd felt like the only person not heading off for one last taste of summer.

He should have been among them. He'd intended to be.

Cullen lifted the bottle to his lips and drank some water. He'd certainly had enough choices.

Las Vegas, for the usual O'Connell end of summer blast. Connecticut, for the barbecue Keir and Cassie were throwing because Cassie was too pregnant for the long flight to Vegas. He had invitations to house parties in the Hamptons, on the Cape, on Martha's Vineyard and half a dozen other places, and there was always the lure of three days at Nantucket.

Instead, he was here in hot and muggy Boston for no good reason except he wasn't in the mood to go anywhere.

Well, except, maybe Berkeley...

Berkeley? Spend Labor Day weekend on one of the campuses of the University of California?

Cullen snorted, finished off the water and dumped the empty bottle in the sink.

Back to square one. Wasn't that the same insane thought he'd had flying home from Fallon's wedding in July? It made no more sense now then it had made then. You thought about the West Coast, you thought about San Francisco. Or Malibu. Maybe a couple of days at Big Sur.

But Berkeley? What for? Nothing but college kids and grad students, protesters and protests, do-gooders and doomsayers. Maybe that vitality was part of why he'd loved the place as a law student, but those years were a decade behind him. He was older. He'd changed. His idea of a great party involved more than take-out pizza and jugs of cheap wine. And, except for a couple of his law school profs, he didn't have friends there anymore.

Okay. There was Marissa Perez. But he could hardly call her a friend. An acquaintance, was what she'd been. Truth was, he didn't "know" her at all, except in the biblical sense of the word, and even if his sisters sometimes glee-fully teased him about being a male chauvinist, he had to admit that sleeping with a woman wasn't the same as knowing her.

Especially if she crept out of your bed before dawn and left you feeling as if you were the only one who'd just spent a night you'd never forget.

Damn it, this was crazy. Why waste time thinking about a woman he'd seen once and would probably never see again? He was starting to behave like one of the attorneys at his firm. Jack was a dedicated fisherman, always talking about the big one that had gotten away. That's what this was starting to sound like. The sad story of Cullen O'Connell and The Woman Who Got Away.

Cullen opened the fridge again. It was empty except for another couple of bottles of water, a half-full container of orange juice and a lump of something that he figured had once been cheese. He made a face, picked up the lump with two fingers and dumped it into the trash.

So much for having breakfast in.

Maybe that was just as well. He'd pull on a T-shirt, put on sneakers, go down to the deli on the corner and get himself something to eat. Solve two problems at once, so to speak; silence his growling belly and do something use-ful, something that would end all this pointless rehashing of the weekend he'd spent with the Perez woman.

Yeah. He'd do that. Later.

Cullen opened the terrace door and stepped into the

morning heat. The little garden below was quiet. Even the birds seemed to have gone elsewhere.

First he'd try thinking about that weekend in detail, concentrating not just on what had happened in bed but on all of it. A dose of cool logic would surely put an end to this nonsense. Sighing, he sank down in a canvas sling back chair, closed his eyes and turned his face to the sun.

His old Tort Law prof, Ian Hutchins, had invited him to fly out and speak to the Law Students' Association. Cullen hadn't much wanted to do it; he had a full caseload and what little free time he could scrounge, he'd been spending on Nantucket, working on his boat. But he liked Hutchins a lot, respected him, so he'd accepted.

A week before Speaker's Weekend, Hutchins had phoned to make last-minute updates to their arrangements.

"I've asked my best student to be your liaison while you're here," he'd said. "Shuttle you around, answer questions—well, you remember how that works, Cullen. You were liaison for us several times while you were a student here."

Cullen remembered it clearly. People called it a plum assignment and, in some ways, it was. The liaison networked with the speaker and drove him or her around in a car owned by the university, which invariably meant it was in a lot better shape than the student's.

Still, it was almost always a pain-in-the-ass job. Pick up the speaker at the airport, drive him or her here, then there, laugh at inane jokes about what it had been like when the speaker was a student on campus. When Ian added that Cullen's liaison would be a woman, he almost groaned.

"Her name," Ian said, "is Marissa Perez. She's a straight-A scholarship student with a brilliant mind. I'm sure you'll enjoy her company."

"I'm sure I will," Cullen had said politely.

What else could he say? Not the truth, that he'd met enough brilliant female scholarship students to know what to expect. Perez would be tall and skinny with a mass of unkempt hair and thick glasses. She'd wear a shapeless black suit and clunky black shoes. And she'd either be so determined to impress him that she'd never shut up or she'd be so awestruck at being in his presence that she'd be tongue-tied.

Wrong on all counts.

The woman standing at the arrivals gate that Friday evening, holding a discreet sign with his name printed on it, was nothing like the woman he'd anticipated. Tall, yes. Lots of hair, yes. And yes, she was wearing a black suit and black shoes.

That was where the resemblance ended.

The mass of hair was a gleaming mass of ebony waves. She'd pinned it up, or tried to, but strands kept escaping, framing a face that was classically beautiful. Gray eyes, chiseled cheekbones, a lush mouth.

Perfect. And when his gaze dropped lower, the package only got better.

Yes, she was tall. But not skinny. Definitely not skinny. The businesslike cut of the black suit couldn't disguise the soft curves of her body. Her breasts were high, her waist slender, her hips sweetly rounded, and not even the ugliest pair of sensible black shoes he'd ever seen could dim the elegance of legs so long he found himself fantasizing about how she'd look wearing nothing but a thong and thigh-high black stockings.

Cullen felt a hot tightening in his belly and a faint sense of regret. The lady was a babe but she might as well have been a bow-wow. There were unwritten rules you followed on these weekends. He did, anyway.

He never hit on the students he met, any more than he mixed business with pleasure in his professional life back home.

Still, as he walked toward her, he liked knowing he'd spend the next couple of days being shuttled around by a woman so easy on the eyes.

"Miss Perez?" he said, his hand extended.

"*Ms*. Perez," she replied politely.

She held out her hand in return. He took it and the brush of skin against skin rocked him to his toes. ZTS, he told himself. The old O'Connell brothers' explanation for what happened when a man met a stunning woman. Zipper Think Syndrome. He looked at the lovely face turned up to his, saw her eyes flash and had the satisfaction of knowing she'd felt the female equivalent of the same thing.

Maybe not. Maybe he'd just imagined it, because an instant later, her expression was as bland as when he'd first spotted her.

"Welcome to Berkeley, Mr. O'Connell."

After that, it was all business. She drove him to his hotel, made polite but impersonal small talk through a standard hotel meal in a crowded dining room, shook his hand at the elevator in the lobby and said good-night.

The next morning, she picked him up at eight, chauffeured him from place to place all day and never once said anything more personal than "Would you like to have lunch now?" She was courteous and pleasant, but when he opened the restaurant door for her—something he saw irritated her—and their hands brushed, it happened again.

The rush of heat. The shock of it. And now he saw it register on her face long enough for him to know damned well it really had happened, though by the time they were seated, she was once again wearing that coolly polite mask.

He watched her order a salad and iced coffee, told the waitress he'd have the same thing, and contemplated what it would take to get that mask to slip.

Minutes later, he had the answer.

When he'd had the dubious honor of shuttling Big Names from place to place, he'd boned up on their most recent cases and on things in the news that he'd figured might interest them.

His Ms. Perez had done the same thing. He could tell from the always-positive, always-polite references she made during the course of the morning. She'd read up on his own work and reached conclusions about his stance on the work of others.

What would happen if he rocked her boat? Their salads arrived and he decided to find out.

"So," he said, with studied nonchalance, "have you been following Sullivan versus Horowitz in Chicago?"

She looked up. "The women suing that manufacturing company for sexual discrimination? Yes. It's fascinating."

Cullen nodded. "What's fascinating is it's obvious the jury's going to find for the plaintiffs. How the defense could allow seven women on a jury hearing a case that involves trumped-up charges of corporate discrimination I'll never—"

Score one. Those gray eyes widened with surprise.

"Trumped up? I don't understand, Mr. O'Connell." Maybe it was score two, or had she simply forgotten to reciprocate on the first name thing?

"It's Cullen. And what don't you understand, Ms. Perez?"

"You said the charges were—"

"They're crap," he said pleasantly. "Shall I be more specific? It's nonsense that a company shouldn't have the right to hire and fire for reasonable cause. The manager of that department should never have loaded it with so many women. Not that I have anything against women, you understand."

He smiled. She didn't. Score three.

"Don't you," she said coldly, and put down her fork. Oh yeah. Definitely, the mask was starting to slip.

"The only reason you believe all that claptrap about affirmative action," he said lazily, "is because you're going to benefit from it. No offense intended, of course."

That had brought a wash of color into her cheeks. It was a stunning contrast—the brush of apricot against her golden skin—and he'd sat there, enjoying the view as much as he was enjoying the knowledge that she was at war with herself.

Was she going to "yes" the honored guest to death, or tell him she thought he was an asshole?

"Hey," he said, pushing a little harder, "you're female, you're Hispanic… Life's going to be good to you, Ms. Perez."

That did it. To his delight, what won was the truth.

"I am a lawyer, like you, or I will be once I pass the bar. And I am an American, also like you. If life is good to me, it'll be because I've worked hard." Ice clung to each syllable. "But that's something you wouldn't understand, Mr. O'Connell, since you never had to do a day of it in your entire, born-with-a-silver-spoon life."

Whoa. The mask hadn't just slipped, it had fallen off. There was real, honest-to-God, fire-breathing life inside his well-mannered, gorgeous gofer.

She sat back, breathing hard. He sat forward, smiling.

"Nice," he said. "Very nice."

"I'll phone Professor Hutchins. He'll arrange for someone else to drive you around for the rest of the time you're here."

"Did you hear me, Ms. Perez? That was a great performance."

"It was the truth."

"Sorry. Wrong choice of words. Mine was the performance. Yours was the real thing. Honest. Emotional. Wouldn't do in a courtroom, letting it all hang out like that, but a really good lawyer should have at least a couple of convictions he or she won't compromise on."

She glared at him. "What are you talking about?"

"I told you. Integrity, Ms. Perez. And fire in the belly. You have both. For a while, I wasn't sure you did."

He picked up his glass of iced coffee and took a long sip. God, he loved the look on her face. Anger. Confusion. Any other place, any other time he'd have used that old cliché, told her she was even more lovely when she was angry, but this wasn't a date, this was what passed for a business meeting in the woolly wilds of academic jurisprudence.

Besides, she'd probably slug him if he said something so trite.

"I don't... What do you mean, you were performing?"

"Monroe versus Allen, Ms. Perez. One of my first big corporate cases—or didn't your research on me go back that far?"

She opened her mouth, shut it again. He could almost see her mind whirring away, sorting facts out of a mental file.

"Mr. O'Connell." She took a breath. "Was this some kind of test?"

Cullen grinned. "You could call it that, yeah, and before you pick up that glass and toss the contents at me, how about considering that you've just had a taste of what you may someday face in the real world? You want to blow up when stuff like that's tossed at you, do it here. Out there, you'll be more effective if you keep what burns inside you. Discretion is always the better part of valor. Opposing attorneys, good ones, search for the weak spot. If they can find it, they use it." He smiled and raised his glass of iced coffee toward her. "Am I forgiven, Ms. Perez?"

She'd hesitated. Then she'd picked up her glass and touched it to his. "It's Marissa," she'd said, and for the first time, she'd flashed a real smile.

Cullen got to his feet, slid open the terrace door and went back into the coolness of the living room.

The rest of the afternoon had passed quickly. They'd talked about law, about law school, about everything under the sun except what happened each time they accidentally touched each other. She'd dropped him at his hotel at five, come back for him at six, driven him to the dinner at which he'd made a speech he figured had gone over well because there'd been smiles, laughter, applause and even rapt concentration.

All he'd been able to concentrate on was Marissa, seated,

as a matter of courtesy, at a table near the dais. No black suit and clunky shoes tonight. She'd worn a long silk gown in a shade of pale rose that made her eyes look like platinum stars; her hair was loose and drawn softly back from her face.

The dress was demure. She wore no makeup that he could see. And yet she was the sexiest woman imaginable, perhaps because she wasn't only beautiful and desirable but because he knew what a fine mind was at work behind that lovely face.

Even though he figured it might kill him, he did the right thing.

He never so much as touched her elbow or her hand during the after-dinner reception and when she drove him back to his hotel for the last time, he sat squarely on his side of the car and kept his eyes on the road instead of on the curve of her thigh visible under the clinging silk of her gown.

"Thank you for everything," he said politely, once they reached the parking lot.

"You're welcome," she said, just as politely, and then, so quickly it still stunned him, everything changed.

To this day, he didn't know what had happened, only that what began as a simple handshake changed into a fevered meeting of mouths and bodies.

"Don't go," he'd whispered, and Marissa had trembled in his arms as she opened her mouth to the searing heat of his.

They'd gone to his room through the back entrance of the hotel because they couldn't stop touching each other and when he undressed her, when he took her to bed...

"Oh man," Cullen muttered, and he stripped off his shorts and headed for the shower again.

THIS time, after he toweled off, he shaved, put on a pair of khakis and a black T-shirt and reached for the telephone.

He needed a change of scene. That was a no-brainer. It

was a little late to make weekend escape plans—the roads would still be crowded—but he knew all the back ways to reach the airport at Nantucket. Yeah. Maybe the best choice was the closest choice.

His cottage, and his boat.

Cullen punched in the number of the couple who took care of the cottage. The woman answered; he asked how she was, how her husband was, how the weather was…and then he heard himself tell her he'd just phoned to touch bases and no, he wouldn't be coming out for the weekend and he hoped they'd have terrific weather and enjoy the three days, et cetera, et cetera, et cetera.

He hit the disconnect button, ran his hand over his face. Okay. Obviously, he wasn't in the mood for a weekend of sailing. Well, what *was* he in the mood for? Something other than rattling around here, that was for sure.

Who to call next? Keir, to ask what time the barbecue was on? His mother, to tell her he'd be home after all? Or should he head for one of those other parties, maybe that one in Malibu? That was a better idea. His family would take one look at him, ask questions he couldn't answer.

Hell.

Cullen grabbed his address book. He'd call the redhead he'd dated a couple of times the past month. She was pretty and lots of fun, and if he hadn't called her in a week or two, it was because he was busy.

He hadn't taken her to bed, either.

How come?

Perhaps this was the weekend to remedy that oversight. The lady had made it very clear she was more than ready to join him in the horizontal rumba.

Cullen smiled, thumbed open the address book, flipped to the page that had her number on it…

"Crap!"

He slammed the book shut, took a quick walk around the room and tried to figure out what in hell was going on.

No sailboat. No gorgeous redhead. What *did* he want to do with the weekend?

The answer came without any hesitation and he acted on it that same way, not fighting it anymore, just grabbing the address book and telephone again, punching in a series of digits before he could change his mind.

"Flyaway Charters," a cheery voice said. "How may we help you?"

"You can tell me how fast you can get me to Berkeley," Cullen said. "Yeah, that's right. Berkeley, California."

CHAPTER THREE

BY THE time the chartered Learjet landed in California, Cullen had come to the conclusion he was crazy.

He'd flown 3,000 miles in six hours, gone from East coast time to Pacific coast time—something that always left him feeling vaguely disoriented—and now, as he stepped onto the tarmac, he was engulfed by air so hot and humid it made the weather he'd left behind seem like an arctic paradise.

And for what?

What in hell was he doing?

He'd never chased after a woman in his life. Well, not since the seventh grade, when he'd made a fool of himself over Trudy Gershwin, but seventh grade was long gone. He wasn't a kid. Neither was Marissa Perez. She was history and so was the night they'd spent in bed.

History? Cullen slung the strap of his carry-on bag over his shoulder as he walked toward the terminal. That night was barely a blip in the fabric of his life. Who gave a damn why she'd slept with him, then vanished and refused to take his calls?

Trouble was, he'd reached that conclusion somewhere over the pastures and fields of the Midwest, a few hours and fifteen hundred miles too late. He'd come within a breath of telling the pilot to turn the jet around.

He'd thought about phoning his brothers. One or the other would give him good advice.

Hey, bro, Sean or Keir would say, *you know what your problem is? You've got a bad case of ZTS.*

Yes, he'd thought, I do. He'd smiled, even reached for the phone…and then he'd realized that first he'd have to tell the whole story, the weekend in California, making a fool of himself with Marissa, the infuriating months since then.

Besides, this wasn't ZTS. He wasn't thinking with his gonads, he simply wanted answers. Closure. The word of the day.

So he'd sat back, finished the flight and now, as he stepped into the welcome chill of the terminal, Cullen told himself he was glad he had.

Closure. Right. That's what he wanted, what he was entitled to, and, by God, he wasn't going home without it.

He found the rental car counter easily enough, managed a "hello" he hoped was civil and slapped the confirmation number of his reservation on the counter.

"Good afternoon, Mr. O'Connell," the clerk said, her smile as bright as if she were about to hand him a winning lottery ticket instead of the keys to…

A four-door sedan? Cullen blinked as he read the paper she slid in front of him.

"There's some mistake here, miss. I reserved a convertible."

The blinding smile dimmed just a little. "I know. But this is a holiday weekend."

"And?"

"And, it's all we have left."

He knew she meant he was lucky to get anything with an engine and four wheels. She was right, too, and really, what did the type of car he drove matter? He wasn't here for a good time; he was on a safari to Egoville because, yeah, the simple truth was this was all about ego. His. The Perez babe had dented it, and he was here to set things right.

Man, acknowledging that nasty truth really put the icing on the cake.

Cullen glared, muttered something about inefficiency as

he signed the papers and scooped up the keys. He started to stalk away but after a couple of steps, he rolled his eyes and turned back toward the counter.

"Sorry," he said in a clipped tone. "I'm in a bad mood, but I didn't mean to take it out on you."

The clerk's smile softened. "It's the weather, sir. Everybody's edgy. What we need is a good soaking rain."

Cullen nodded. What *he* needed was a good soaking for his head. If he'd done that in the first place, he'd still be back home. Since it was too late for that, he settled for buying an extra-large container of coffee, black, at a stand near the exit door. Maybe part of the problem was that he was still operating on East coast time. Pumping some caffeine through his system might help.

It didn't.

The coffee tasted as if somebody had washed their socks in it. He dumped it in a trash bin after one sip. And the sedan was a color that could only be called bilious-green. Five minutes on the freeway toward Berkeley and Cullen knew it also had all the vitality of a sick sloth.

Not a good beginning for a trip he probably shouldn't have made.

Cullen fell in behind an ancient truck whose sole reason for existence was to make green sedans feel like Ferraris.

Beggars couldn't be choosers.

His hands tightened on the steering wheel.

And that was the one thing he wouldn't do with Perez. Beg. No way. He'd confront her, get in her face if that's what it took, and he wouldn't let her off the hook until she explained herself, but he wouldn't let her think he was pleading for answers…

Even if he was.

Damn it, he was entitled to answers! A woman didn't give a man the brush-off after a night like the one they'd spent. All that heat. Her little cries. The way she'd responded to him, the way she'd touched him, as if every caress was a first-time exploration. And the look on her face, the way her eyes had blurred when he took her up over the edge...

Had it all been a game? Lies, deceit, whatever a woman might call pretending she was feeling something in a man's arms when she really wasn't?

Cullen hit the horn, cursed, swung into the passing lane and chugged along beside the wheezing truck until he finally overtook it.

Whether she liked it or not, Marissa Perez was going to talk to him.

He had her address—she'd never given it to him but he'd found it easily by using her phone number to do a reverse search on the Internet. Another exit...yes, there it was.

Cullen took the ramp and wound through half a dozen streets in a neighborhood he remembered from his own graduate days. It was still the same: a little shabby around the edges but, all in all, safe and pleasant. He'd wondered what kind of area she lived in, whether it was okay or dangerous or what.

He hadn't liked imagining her in a rundown house on a dark street. Not that it was any of his concern.

"What the hell's with you, O'Connell?" he muttered, digging her address from his pocket. "You thinking of turning into the Good Fairy?"

Her building was on the corner. Cullen parked, trotted up the steps to a wide stoop and checked the names below the buzzers in the cramped entry. No Perez. He checked again, frowned, then pressed the button marked Building Manager.

"Yes?"

A tinny voice came over the speaker. Cullen leaned in.

"I'm looking for Marissa Perez's apartment."

"She don't live here."

He glanced at the slip of paper in his hand. "Isn't this 345 Spring Street?"

"She used to live here, but she moved."

"Moved where? Do you have her new address?"

"I got no idea."

"But she must have left a forwarding—"

Click. Cullen was talking to the air. "Damn," he muttered, heading back to his car while he took his cell phone from his pocket. He hadn't intended to call. Why give her advance notice of his visit? Now, he had no choice.

And no success, either.

"The number you have reached, 555-1157, is no longer in service."

He tried again, got the same message. What was going on here? Cullen called the operator and asked for a phone number for Marissa Perez.

There was none. Not a public listing, anyway.

Annoyed, he tossed the cell phone aside. There wasn't a way in the world he could shake loose a privately listed number from the phone company. Back home, maybe, he could pull some strings, but not here.

Someone had to have her number or her address. The bursar's office, the dean's office…

Or her advisor. Ian Hutchins.

Cullen sat back and drummed his fingertips on the steering wheel. The offices would be closed for the weekend. Ian was the logical choice, but he'd want to know why Cullen was trying to get in touch with Marissa.

He was digging himself in deeper and deeper.

A sane man would turn around and head for home but then, a sane man wouldn't have come out here in the first place.

He started the car. It lurched forward. The engine bitched when he tried to coax more speed from it, but it finally gave a couple of hiccups and complied.

Even the car knew he wasn't in a mood to be screwed with, he thought grimly.

He only hoped the Perez babe could read him just as quickly.

THE Hutchinses lived in a big Victorian on a tree-lined street in North Oakland.

Music, and the sound of voices and laughter, spilled from the yard behind the house. The air was pungent with the mingled aromas of smoking charcoal, lager beer and grilling beef.

Cullen climbed the porch steps, took a deep breath and rang the bell. After a minute, Hutchins's wife, Sylvia, opened the door.

"Hello," she said, her lips curving into a cautious smile that suddenly turned genuine. "Cullen O'Connell! What a nice surprise."

"Hello, Sylvia. Sorry to barge in without notice, but—"

"Don't be silly!" Laughing, she took his arm and drew him inside the foyer. "I was afraid you were the fire marshal. Ian's grilling steaks."

Cullen chuckled. "The Hutchins method of incineration. Nothing's changed, huh?"

"Not a thing," Sylvia said cheerfully. "Come inside, Cullen. I had no idea you were in town. Ian never said a word."

"He doesn't know. And I apologize again for not phoning first. You have guests."

"We have half the Bay area, you mean. You know these barbecues of Ian's—students, faculty, friends, every person he's ever met on the street. Besides, why would you call first? You're always welcome. Let me get you a drink and introduce you around."

"Actually, I just need a couple of minutes of Ian's time."

"Oh, come on. There are a couple of unattached women here—Ian's third-and fourth-year students—I'm sure would love to meet you."

"Is Marissa Perez one of them?" *Holy hell.* How had that slipped out? Cullen felt his face burn. "I met her that last time I was out here. She drove me around all weekend."

Sylvia arched an eyebrow. "Marissa? No, she's not here. Come to think of it, I haven't seen her in a while." She winked. "I'm sure we can find a replacement."

"Sylvia," Cullen said quietly, "if you'd just tell Ian I'm here... I need to ask him something and then I'll be on my way."

"Ah. You're really not in a party mood, are you?" Smiling, she patted his hand. "I'll get Ian. Why don't you wait in his study?"

Cullen bent and kissed her cheek. "Thanks."

The professor's study was a small room off the foyer. Cullen had always liked it. An old sofa covered in flowered chintz faced a small fireplace; an antique cherry desk stood in a corner. The walls were hung with family photos, and an ancient Oriental rug lent a mellow touch to the hardwood floor.

The place felt familiar and comforting. And when Ian Hutchins crossed the threshold with a beer in either hand, Cullen smiled.

"As always," he said, taking a glass from Hutchins, "the perfect host."

"It's not the fatted calf—I've got that laid out on the barbecue—but I figured you might be thirsty." The men shook hands, then sat down. "If I'd known you were going to be in town—"

"It was a last minute decision."

"And Sylvia tells me you can't stay for our party."

"No. I'm sorry, I can't. I'm just passing through and I wondered..." *Get to it, O'Connell.* "Remember when I was here to give that speech?"

"Of course. We had a lot of excellent feedback. Matter of fact, I was going to give you a call, see if you'd be interested in—"

"The woman who was my liaison. Marissa Perez."

Hutchins cocked his head. "Yes?"

"I'm trying to get in touch with her." Cullen cleared his

throat. "Turns out she's moved. I thought you might have her new address."

"May I ask why you're trying to contact Ms. Perez, Cullen?"

Cullen stared at the older man, then rose to his feet. He put his untouched glass of beer on a table and tucked his hands into the pockets of his trousers.

"It's a personal matter."

"Personal."

"Ms. Perez and I had a misunderstanding, and I'd like to clear the air."

"How personal? What sort of misunderstanding?"

Cullen's mouth narrowed. "Excuse me?"

"I said—"

"I heard what you said, Ian. And, frankly, I don't see that it's any of your business."

Hutchins put down his glass, too, and got to his feet. "Easy, Cullen. I'm not trying to pry, but, well, I owe a certain amount of confidentiality to my students. I'm sure you understand that."

"Hell, I'm not asking you to tell me her social security number!" *Easy*, Cullen told himself. *Just take it nice and slow.* "Look, I want to talk to her, that's all. If you're not comfortable giving me her address, then give me her phone number. Her new one's unlisted."

Hutchins sighed. "Is it? Well, I'm not surprised. All in all, Marissa seems to have done her best to sever all her university relationships."

"Why? What's going on? Did she transfer out?"

"Worse. She quit. And I'm worried about her."

"What do you mean, she quit? You said she was one of your best students. Why would she quit?"

"She wasn't *one* of my best, she was *the* best. I don't know why she withdrew from school. She began behaving strangely, is all I know, and made what I think are some poor decisions, but..." Hutchins took a deep breath, then slowly expelled it. "That's why I was questioning you,

Cullen. I figured, if you and she had become friends, perhaps it would be all right to share my concerns with you.''

"Ian, you've known me for years. You know you can count on me to be discreet.''

Hutchins nodded. "Very well, then. Here's the situation. Marissa's walked away from a promising future. I know that sounds melodramatic but it's true. She was to edit *Law Review* next year and after graduation, she was slated to clerk for Judge Landers.'' He spread his hands. "She's turned her back on all of it.''

"Why? What happened to her? Drugs? Alcohol?'' Cullen could hear the roughness in his own voice. He cleared his throat and flashed a quick smile. "We can't afford to let the smart ones get away, Ian. There must be a reason.''

"I'm sure there is, but she wouldn't discuss it. I tried to talk to her the first time I realized something was wrong. She flunked one of my exams.'' Hutchins gave a sharp laugh. "Understand, she never so much as gave a wrong answer until then. Anyway, I called her in for a chat. I asked if she had a problem she wanted to discuss with me. She said she didn't.''

"And?''

"And, because I was her advisor, I began hearing from her other instructors. The same thing was happening in their classes. She was failing tests, not turning in papers, not participating in discussions. They all asked if I knew the reason.''

"So, you spoke with Marissa again…''

"Of course. She told me she'd had to take on a heavier work schedule at some restaurant. The Chiliburger, I think she said, over on Telegraph. I offered to see about some additional scholarship money but she said no, she had expenses that would extend beyond the school year.'' Hutchins frowned. "She looked awful, Cullen. Tired. Peaked, if you'll pardon such an old-fashioned word. I asked her if she was sick. She said she wasn't.'' Hutchins shrugged. "Next thing I knew, she'd dropped out of school.

I phoned her, got the same message I assume you got. I even went to her apartment, but she'd cleared out."

"Did you go to this place where she works? The Chiliburger?"

"No. This is America," Ian said with a little smile. "People are entitled to lead their lives as they wish. Marissa had made it clear she didn't want to discuss her problems. I'm her advisor, not her father. There's a certain line I don't have the right to cross."

Cullen could feel a muscle knotting and unknotting in his jaw. Hutchins was right. Marissa Perez was entitled to lead her life as she saw fit. If she wanted to sleep with a stranger and then ignore him, she could. If she wanted to drop out of law school and walk away from a future others would kill for, she could do that, too.

And he could do what he had to do. Find her, and find out what in hell was going on.

"You're right," Cullen said as the men walked slowly to the front door. "You did everything you could."

"You're going to talk with her? Assuming you can find her, that is?"

Cullen laughed. "I have a feeling finding her won't be hard. Getting her to talk to me might be a different story."

CULLEN knew exactly where to find the Chiliburger. It was, as burger joints went, an institution.

He had eaten countless fries and burgers within the confines of its greasy walls; he'd studied in its vinyl booths, at wooden tables scarred with the incised initials of at least four decades' worth of students.

He drove to the restaurant, lucked out on a parking space and strolled inside. A blast of heavy-metal music made him wince. Even the stuff pouring from the jukebox was the same. So was the aroma of fried onions, chili and beer.

He scanned the room. It was crowded. No surprise there, either. Holiday or not, there were always some students who remained in town. It was coming up on supper time, and they'd gather at places like this for a cheap meal and some laughs.

He spotted a vacant booth way in the back, went to it and slid across the red imitation leather seat. The table was still littered with plates and glasses; he pushed them aside and reached for the stained menu propped between the ketchup bottle and the salt and pepper shakers.

As far as he could tell, only one waitress was working the tables, a heavyset blonde of indeterminate age.

No Marissa.

After a while, the blonde appeared at his elbow and shifted a wad of gum from one side of her mouth to the other.

"You know what you want or you need more time?"

"A Coke, please."

"That's it?"

Cullen smiled. What she meant was, *You're going to take up space at one of my tables and that's all you're going to spend?*

"And a burger. The house special, medium-well." He shoved the menu back into its hiding place, considered asking Blondie about Marissa and decided this wasn't the right time. "No rush."

"No rush is right. I got all these tables to handle by myself."

"Nobody else on with you tonight?"

"Oh, there's somebody on with me." Blondie rolled her eyes. "She just isn't here yet, is all."

Cullen tried not to show his sudden interest. "She's late?"

"She's always late," Blondie said. "Last couple months, anyway. You want guacamole or mayo on that burger?"

"You pick it. How come?"

"How come what?"

"How come the other waitress started showing up late?"

Blondie shrugged. "How would I know? Only thing I'm

sure of is that it's a pain in the butt, trying to cover for her so the boss doesn't realize she's not here."

"Then why do it?"

The waitress's expression softened and she leaned toward him. "'Cause she's a nice kid. Always did her fair share until now."

"And that changed?"

"It sure did. She says she's just been feeling under the weather." The blonde shifted her gum. "You ask me," she said slyly, "the trouble with her is that she's—"

"She's what?"

Something in his tone must have given him away. Blondie drew back. "What's with all these questions?"

"I'm just making conversation, that's all."

"Well, you got questions about Marissa Perez, ask her direct. She just came in. I'll put your order in, but it'll be her takes care of— Mister? Mister, what's the problem?"

What was the problem? Cullen didn't know where to begin. Marissa was coming from behind the counter that ran the length of one side of the room, but this wasn't the Marissa he'd spent countless nights dreaming about.

Her face was devoid of color; there were rings under her eyes. Her hair, which he remembered as being as lustrous as a crow's wing, was dull and lifeless.

Something was terribly wrong with her.

He shot to his feet.

She saw him as he did.

She paled—though how she could get paler than she already was, he thought grimly, was hard to comprehend. He saw her lips form his name as she took a step back.

"Marissa," he said, but he knew she couldn't hear him, not over the din of music and loud voices.

She stared at him. Her lips formed his name. For a second, he thought she was going to pass out. He mouthed an oath, took a step toward her, but she pasted a bloodless smile to her lips and started toward him.

"Cullen," she said in a thin voice, "what a nice surprise."

It didn't take a genius to know that her smile was a lie. She was surprised, all right, but nice? No way. She was about as glad to see him as a lone gazelle would be to see a lion.

"Yeah," he said coldly, "what a nice surprise." His hand closed around her wrist. "You look terrible."

"Are you always so free with compliments?"

"Cut the crap." Why was he so angry? So what if she looked like death warmed over? It wasn't his business, he told himself, even as his eyes narrowed and drilled into hers. "Is that why you didn't call me? Have you been sick?"

"I didn't call you because I didn't want to call you. I know that must come as a shock, Cullen, but—"

"Is that the reason you left school?"

Her face colored. "Who told you that?"

"You were the best student Ian Hutchins had, and you quit. You moved out of your apartment, you're working your tail off in a joint like this and you look like hell. I want to know why."

"Just who do you think you are, Mr. O'Connell? I don't owe any explanations to you or anybody. My life is my—"

"I'm making it my business. Last time we saw each other, you had the world by the tail. I want to know what happened."

"But you're not going to find out. I told you, I don't have to— Hey. Hey, what do you think you're doing?"

Cullen was tugging her toward the door. Marissa tried to dig in her heels, but he paid no attention.

"Stop it!" she said in a frantic whisper. "Are you crazy? You'll cost me my job!"

"Tell her you're taking a break to talk to an old friend," he growled when Blondie hurried toward them.

"Marissa? You okay? You want me to call the cops?"

And turn this bad dream into a full-fledged nightmare?

"No," Marissa said quickly, "No, I'm fine. I'm just—I'm taking a break…"

The next thing she knew, she was tucked in the passenger seat of Cullen's car and they were pulling away from the curb and into traffic.

CHAPTER FOUR

MARISSA swung toward Cullen.

"Are you insane?" Her voice rose until it was a shriek. "Take me back! Turn this car around and take me—"

"Buckle your seat belt."

"You son of a bitch! Did you hear what I said?" She lunged toward him and slammed her fist into his shoulder. "Take-me-back!"

Cullen took one hand from the steering wheel and wrapped it around hers.

"You want to hit me, wait until we stop moving. For now, keep your hands to yourself. And put on that belt."

She stared at him. His profile looked as if it had been chiseled from stone. He was driving fast, weaving in and out of traffic, and she knew she had about as much chance of getting him to take her back to the Chiliburger as she had of changing what happened the weekend they'd met.

You couldn't turn back time.

Marissa lay a hand protectively over her belly. Then she clipped the ends of her seat belt together.

Given the chance, she wasn't even sure she would turn it back. At first, oh God, at first, she'd have given anything to erase that night but now—now, things had changed. She'd faced what had happened, gone from hating the changes in her life to hating only herself for her weakness and stupidity, for making the same mistakes her mother had made...

No.

She took a deep breath.

She wasn't going there. All that was behind her and, anyway, it had nothing to do with the man sitting beside her except in the most fundamental way. Besides, why was she wasting time on this nonsense? She had more immediate concerns. Her job. She'd come in late again, and two minutes later, Cullen had dragged her away. Would Tony take her back? He would. He *had* to. She'd beg. She'd grovel, if that was what it took. She needed the money desperately.

How would a man like Cullen O'Connell, born to wealth and power, ever understand that?

She'd tell Tony that Cullen was an old boyfriend. That he'd just gotten in from out of town. She'd laugh, make it seem as if it was all about being macho. That was true enough. Cullen did have a macho quality. Tony thought he had one, too, but it wasn't the same. Cullen's was the kind some women found attractive.

All right. *She'd* found it attractive, but that didn't give him the right to swagger into her life and take over. As for telling him why she'd quit school, changed all her plans...that wasn't going to happen.

The only way to handle him would be to play on that machismo. Make him think she saw his high-handed interference as gallantry, and that she appreciated it even if it had been misplaced.

Marissa cleared her throat.

"Look, I appreciate your concern, but—"

"What street?"

"What?"

"I said, what street do you live on? I'm taking you home."

"No," she said quickly, "you're not. You're taking me back to the Chiliburger."

"You want to give me your address, or you want to drive in circles until we run out of gas?" He looked at her as they stopped at a red light. "Your choice, lady."

Lady. The way he said it turned the word into something vaguely impolite. So much for finding a way to handle him.

"I don't think you understand," she said, trying to stay calm. "I need that job."

"You have a bachelor's degree and three years of law school." He smiled sardonically as he stepped on the gas. "Oh yeah. Right. I'll just bet you sure as hell need a job serving burgers and fries."

"How readily you jump to conclusions, Mr. O'Connell. I have a degree in political science. Do you see anybody clamoring for my services? As for three years of law school… 'Sorry, Miss Perez,'" she said in a high-pitched voice, "'but we really don't have any openings in our office for paralegals.'" She looked at Cullen, eyes flashing dangerously. "Translation. 'Are you kidding? Why would our attorneys want to work with a clerk who probably thinks she knows everything?'"

"Okay. So getting a good job would be tough."

Marissa sank back in her seat and folded her arms. "Something like that," she said tonelessly.

"What about your scholarship money?"

"What scholarship money?"

"Ian Hutchins says—"

"I *had* a scholarship. You have to attend school full-time to keep it."

"And?"

Look how he'd drawn her into this discussion! Marissa blew back the hair that had fallen over her forehead.

"And," she said coolly, "this conversation is over."

They sat in silence for a few seconds. Then Cullen looked at her.

"I'm still waiting. Where do you live?"

"None of your business. How many times do I have to tell you that? Take me back to the Chiliburger."

"Yeah, I'll bet your boss would like that. What's he do, work you twelve hours a day?"

"Tony agreed to give me extra hours, yes."

"What a prince," Cullen said sarcastically. "Hasn't he noticed you look like you're going to fall on your face any minute?"

Marissa almost laughed. Tony probably had no idea what she looked like. She was a waitress, a commodity about as invisible in a place like the Chiliburger as the film of old grease on the griddle.

But she wasn't going to tell that to Cullen. She wasn't going to tell him anything. She'd made that decision months ago.

She could take care of herself. She always had…except for that night. How could it have happened? Hadn't she learned anything, growing up?

Some girls' mothers taught them to cook or sew.

Hers had taught her the truth about men, and life.

The day she got her first period, her mother handed her a box of tampons and a bucket of advice.

"You're a woman now, Mari," she'd said. "Men will look at you, but don't you let 'em come near you. They're all like the son of a bitch planted you inside me, gruntin' between your legs, then zippin' up their pants and walkin' away. The rest is your problem. You remember that, girl. Nothin' lasts, especially if you're dumb enough to hope it will."

She always had remembered, until Cullen. How come? Was it because her mother had omitted one salient bit of advice, that when a man took your breath away, he took away your ability to think?

That's what had happened to her. Cullen had taken her breath away. One look, and she'd been lost. He was so ruggedly handsome, so funny, so smart…and each time their hands accidentally brushed, it seemed as if a bolt of electricity sizzled straight through her bones.

No matter. She wasn't her mother, despite what had happened. *She* wouldn't confront a man who was little more than a stranger with a truth he wouldn't want to hear. She wouldn't beg him to believe her. She knew how things would go if a woman named Perez tried to tell a man like Cullen O'Connell that he'd played a role in a sad little tragedy that was really of her own making.

Her fault, all of it.

She should have been strong enough to ignore the hot attraction between them instead of melting into his kiss. And when he'd asked if she had protection just before he undressed her, she should have remembered that though she took the pill to regulate her period, she'd been off it the start of the month because she had the flu.

Marissa closed her eyes.

Oh yes, she should have remembered...but how could she, when she'd wanted him so badly? When the taste of his mouth, the touch of his hands, drove her wild? Lost. She'd been lost—

"...that address but hey, what's the point? There are worse things than spending the night driving around the Bay."

Marissa opened her eyes. They were heading for the water and the bridge across it, getting farther and farther from the Chiliburger. For all she knew, Tony had already lined up someone to replace her.

"This is ridiculous," she said sharply. "Don't you ever give up?"

"No," Cullen said, just as sharply, "I don't."

There was a warning in his words, but she decided to ignore it. If she played along, he'd go away.

Back to Plan A, and letting Mr. Macho think he'd won.

"All right. Drive me home, if that's what it takes to get you out of my face."

"A charming image."

"I'm not interested in charm, Mr. O'Connell. I just want to get rid of you. Make a U-turn, then take a right at the first light."

He nodded and did as she'd told him. Marissa let out a pent-up breath. Just a little while longer and she'd be back at the Chiliburger. Except for her latenesses the past few weeks, she was a damned good waitress. Tony would take her back. He had to.

She needed her job. How else would she be able to put away enough money to have her baby?

The baby she would love, as her mother had never loved her.

The baby Cullen O'Connell had fathered.

CULLEN couldn't believe where her directions took him.

He slowed the car and stared out the window. The houses that lined the street looked as if they were only a couple of weeks away from being condemned. A bunch of kids wearing what he figured were gang colors lounged against a graffiti-scarred brick wall; a scrawny dog pawed through a spilled bag of rotting garbage near the curb.

"This is where you live?"

"You can stop in the middle of the block."

Well, that was definitely the answer to his question. "This isn't exactly a garden spot."

"Oh, but that's the reason I chose it. I didn't want to be bothered by photographers from Showplace Homes."

Marissa's tone was as cool as his. She was still pale but the angle of her jaw told him she'd regained some of her composure. So would he, as soon as he dropped her off. He still wasn't sure why he'd carried her out of that miserable dive. So what if something had gone wrong in her life?

She was right. It wasn't his problem.

Still, he might be able to help her. He'd helped other students. Ian called him once in a while, asking if he had any contacts who could offer a job to a recent graduate, or if he knew anybody who was taking on interns for the summer. He could do as much for Marissa. All he had to do was get her to talk to him, tell him what the trouble was.

Cullen frowned as he pulled to the curb in front of a four-story building that looked little better than the rest on the street.

On the other hand, she didn't want help. She didn't want anything from him. And that was fine. Two people, one spring night. It wasn't exactly a memory to tuck into a journal.

Okay. He'd sit here, wait until she went inside, let her sashay across from the gang-bangers and the pile of rags stirring in a nearby doorway.

Sure he would.

Cullen reached for the door. No man would let a woman walk alone on a street like this.

"I'll see you inside."

"That's not necessary."

"Yeah, it is. Those kids don't look much like Boy Scouts."

"No! Really?"

She fluttered her lashes with such innocence that he had to laugh. For a moment, the tension between them eased. Her lips curved in the start of a smile and he remembered how soft her mouth was, how sweet it tasted. Their eyes met; she was remembering, too.

Then, why hadn't she returned his calls?

He sprang from the car and made it to the sidewalk just as she stepped onto it.

"I'm walking you in," he said grimly. "And if you give me a hard time about it, we'll have a repeat of our exit from the Chiliburger."

She shot him a look of pure venom. He ignored it and walked her to the broken concrete steps that led to her front door. He started to ask for her keys, but why would you need keys when there was a hole where the lock should have been?

"I can't believe you live in a place like this," he said curtly.

Her response was just as curt. "I can't believe you think it's any of your business."

Right again, he thought. Nothing about her was his business. Nothing...except the answers he'd come for and had yet to get. He caught her by the shoulders as she pushed open the door.

"Just tell me one thing," he said roughly. "Why didn't you answer my calls?"

Two spots of color stained her pale cheeks, but her response was swift. Only a tremor in her voice told him he'd caught her off guard.

"I didn't see much point in it. We both knew we weren't going to see each other again."

"You knew that, huh?" His tone was harsh. "Then, how come I didn't?"

"It was a logical conclusion. You live in the east, I live here. The odds on us getting together were—"

"So, what was that night? Just a casual roll in the hay?" She flinched, but he wasn't about to stop now, not when he'd been carrying all this anger inside him for so long. "Is that your style? Go to bed with a guy and forget about him the next morning?"

The crimson in her cheeks suffused her entire face. He felt her arm jerk and he knew she was going to slug him, but before she could, he clamped his hand around her wrist.

"You get the hell out of my life!"

"Answer my question first."

"I'm not answering anything." Fury danced in her eyes. "Get away from me or I'll scream."

Cullen laughed. "And that's going to bring the good citizens of this fine neighborhood running, right?" His face turned hard; he let go of her and slapped his hand against the door. "Trust me, Ms. Perez. I'm as eager to see the last of you as you are to see the last of me. We get to your apartment, I'm out of here."

Marissa stared at him. Then she turned on her heel, marched into a narrow vestibule perfumed by cabbage, cheap wine and urine, and started up the stairs.

Two floors. Three. She never paused for breath until they reached the fourth-floor landing. Then she turned to him. Her face was pale again, her breathing rapid.

Cullen felt a twinge of alarm.

"Are you okay?"

"I'm fine. And this is where we part company."

"Maybe you should see a doctor."

"Maybe you should give the advice bit a rest."

Her tone was flippant, but it didn't fool him. Something was wrong. Very wrong. Cullen narrowed his eyes on her face.

"Ian thinks you might be sick. Are you?"

"My health isn't—"

"My business. Yeah, I know." He looked past her, at the scarred and dented door that led to her apartment, and something tightened deep inside him. What was she doing here? He wanted answers. Better ones than he'd gotten so far. "That was a steep climb. How about a cup of coffee before you send me on my way?"

"How about you just go?"

His mouth thinned. Marissa Perez was really getting to him. He thought about hauling her into his arms and kissing her. Maybe then she'd drop this disguise of cool disinterest.

No. He wouldn't do that. He wouldn't give her an excuse to tell him he was a fool when he knew it already.

"I'll settle for a glass of iced water."

She folded her arms. He could see the "no" forming on her lips, but something unexpected changed her mind. A door creaked open; a woman in a dingy slip peered at them.

"Oh," she said brightly, "sorry. I thought it was someone for me."

The door swung shut, but not quite all the way. Clearly, they had an audience.

Marissa muttered something, then dug in her pocket for her keys. When her door swung open, she jerked her chin and Cullen stepped past her. As soon as they were inside, she slammed the door and confronted him.

"All right," she snapped, her hands on her hips, her face turned up to his. "What's it going to take to get rid of you? What do you want?"

"I told you. Some water. I'm winded."

Marissa's eyes narrowed. Did Cullen O'Connell think she was stupid? He wasn't even breathing hard. Four flights of steps were nothing to him. She still remembered how hard his body was, that six-pack abdomen, those knotted muscles in his shoulders and arms.

He was up to something, but what? Was he here at Professor Hutchins's request to try and find out why she'd left school? That would really be a laugh. As if she'd tell Cullen, of all people, what had happened to her. That she was carrying his child. Lesson one, learned at her mother's knee: getting a woman pregnant didn't mean a man was a father.

She swung away from him, hurried into the kitchen and returned with a glass of water. He was standing where she'd left him, staring at the peeling walls, the sagging furniture, the worn linoleum.

"Here's your water." He didn't respond and she shoved the glass at him. "I'd appreciate it if you'd drink up and leave."

"Why?"

His voice was sharp, his eyes narrowed as they focused on hers, and she knew his one-word question didn't have a thing to do with what she'd said.

It was safer to pretend it had.

"Because I have things to do, that's why."

"Damn it, Marissa!" He put down the glass. He'd had it with being circumspect, with telling himself whatever was going on here was none of his business. He'd come for closure and found a dozen new questions instead, and he wasn't going home until he had answers. "Forget the games," he said, clasping her shoulders. "I want to know what you're doing in a dump like this."

He felt a tremor race through her body, but her eyes were steady on his.

"I live here. If it's not to you're liking, that's just too—"

"Hutchins says you've given up everything. *Law Re-*

view. The clerkship.'' His mouth twisted. ''Your last year of school. And for what? So you can live in a place that's about ready to be torn down? Work yourself to death at a joint like the Chiliburger?'' She winced as his fingers bit into her flesh. ''Tell me the truth, damn it. Are you sick? Do you need money? Tell me. I'll help you.''

''I don't need your help. And I resent your interference. This is my life. I can live it any way I—''

Cullen cursed, hauled her to her toes and covered her mouth with his. It was what he'd dreamed about, all these months; what he wanted even now, when she'd done everything possible to fuel his anger.

''No,'' she gasped, and pulled away, but he took her face in his hands, knotted one hand in her hair and kissed her again and again until, all at once, she gave a little sob of surrender, sank against him, opened her mouth to his and wrapped her arms around his neck.

Here it was again. That incredible heat. Desire, erupting like a volcano that had been slumbering under a cover of clouds. He wanted her as he'd wanted her that night, as he'd never wanted another woman.

''Marissa,'' he whispered. She sighed his name against his lips and he deepened the kiss, tasting the sweetness he'd never forgotten, drinking it in as if it might assuage his endless thirst for her.

His hand stroked down the length of her spine, traced the delicate vertebrae, slid under her loose shirt and found the ripeness of her breast. Her breath sighed into his mouth as he cupped it, swept the tips of his fingers over the tightly furled nipple.

''Marissa,'' he said again, and she rose on her toes, pressed herself against him as he moved his hand lower, spread his fingers over her belly.

Her gently rounded belly.

Rounded, as his sister-in-law's had been the day he'd driven to the vineyard she and Keir owned, early in Cassie's pregnancy.

Want to say hello to your nephew? Cassie had asked him, and she'd taken his hand, spread it over her stomach...

Cullen went still. He lifted his head, stared down at Marissa, saw her pinched face, her shadowed eyes.

"My God," he said hoarsely. "You're not sick. You're pregnant."

Marissa cried out and pushed free of his arms.

God, what had she done? She'd lost herself, lost the ability to think. The same thing had happened that night she'd slept with this man. She'd forgotten everything then. Her morals. The code she lived by.

Only this was far worse. What she'd forgotten this time was the secret she could never share with him.

"Go away," she whispered shakily.

"Not until I have an answer!" Cullen grabbed her and shook her. "Are you pregnant?"

"No. I'm not. I'm not!"

"Don't lie to me, damn it! That's why you quit school." He let go of her, afraid of what he'd say, what he'd do. She'd given up everything for, what, a moment's foolishness with some man who didn't care enough about her to hang around and take care of her?

When?

When had it happened? His hands closed into fists. Was that why she'd left his bed that night? Because another man was waiting for her? Had she belonged to someone else, even then?

"Who is he?" he said, his words soft and cold. "And where is he? Why is he letting you go through this alone?"

Marissa sank her teeth into her bottom lip. She turned away from Cullen's accusing face. Despite the blistering heat trapped in the airless confines of her ugly apartment, she was shivering.

"Go away," she whispered.

Cullen's hands closed on her shoulders and he swung her toward him. "I'm right, aren't I? He's letting you face this alone. Does he even know what's happened to you? That you've given up the law, that you're sick—"

"I'm not sick," she said fiercely. "I'm pregnant! And I don't need anyone's help! I'm doing just fine on my own."

"Did he abandon you?"

"Abandon…?" Marissa made a sound that was not quite a laugh. How could a man abandon you after a one-night stand? Her mother had always referred to what had happened in her own life as an affair, but Marissa was a realist. One night didn't make for anything but sex. "No. The man who—the man I slept with doesn't know about this."

"Why the hell not?"

"I told you. Because I can handle it myself." She shook free of his hands. "For the last time, Cullen. This doesn't concern you."

Cullen opened his mouth, then closed it. She was right again. It didn't. She was pregnant, she was going to ruin her life, but so what? He had no stake in any of it.

Except for one thing.

"You're right. What you do isn't my affair." His voice roughened. "I just have one last question."

"Don't you get it? I'm not answering any more questions."

"Did you go to him that night?" A muscle knotted in his jaw. "Was that the reason you left my bed? So you could be with him?"

The accusation sliced through her like a knife. She didn't think, she reacted. Her hand flew through the air; she slapped his face with all the strength and despair so long constricting her heart.

The sound reverberated through the silent room; Cullen's head snapped back but it didn't stop him from snarling a curse, grabbing her wrist and yanking her hand behind her back.

"Answer me. Did you sleep with him that same night?"

"No!"

"First me. Then him. The man who was waiting for you.

Your lover. You left me so you could go to him, your body still warm from mine, your mouth still swollen with my kisses—''

''I don't have a lover. I *never* had a lover. I've never been with a man in my life except—''

She moaned, clamped her lips together. But it was too late. God, too late!

Silence. Endless seconds of it, ticking into the airless room. Marissa turned away and shut her eyes. After an eternity, Cullen spoke in a hoarse whisper.

''Are you telling me the child in your womb is mine?''

It still wasn't too late to lie. She could say she'd misspoken or he'd misunderstood.

''Marissa.'' Cullen turned her toward him. ''Marissa. Look at me.''

She shook her head. He put his hand under her chin and raised her face until their eyes met.

''I want the truth.'' His voice was flat. ''Now, or in a courtroom. Your choice. Am I the man who made you pregnant?''

She knew the warning was real. Cullen wasn't a man who'd make an idle threat. Her stomach was churning. This was exactly the kind of confrontation she'd dreaded.

Still, it had happened. And now that it had, what difference could it possibly make? Once he knew the truth, he'd stop all the fancy talk about some man letting her face this alone. That was okay, too, because once he understood that she wanted nothing from him, he'd be out of her life forever.

''Answer me,'' Cullen snapped. ''Is this child mine?''

Marissa took a deep breath. And said yes.

CHAPTER FIVE

ONE of the best things about growing up an O'Connell was having brothers and sisters who knew you almost as well as you knew yourself.

Forget "almost," Cullen thought as he sat across from his brother, Sean, in a Boston steakhouse. Truth was, his family, especially Keir and Sean, knew him about as well as he knew himself.

Maybe better.

That was a good thing when you were, say, sitting at a bar, eyeing women, rating them on the O'Connell scale. The old Zipper Think Syndrome. Not that Keir played the game with them anymore but there was a time a woman would walk through the door, stroll past them and they'd all look at each other and know precisely where the lady placed for each of them on the ZTS scale.

Yeah, but there were other times when the last thing a man wanted was to have someone else, even his brother, *especially* his brother, inside his head.

Cullen picked up his glass of ale.

Right now, Sean was doing his best to read his mind. Cullen could tell by the glint in his brother's eye. So far, the kid hadn't come up with anything—how could he, when the facts were so incredible? But Sean had definitely tuned in to both his mood, which was low, and his disposition, which bordered on ugly.

Now, Sean was trying his damnedest to improve things, telling a story that involved him, a Greek shipowner, an Italian prince, and a Hollywood sex goddess. Sean had the

Gaelic gift for gab and a terrific sense of humor, meaning the story was probably funny as hell and definitely intriguing.

Assuming a man was in the right mood.

Cullen wasn't.

How could he be? His life would never be the same again. He was still trying to come to grips with what had happened. The truth of it was, he doubted that he ever could.

Marissa Perez was pregnant.

No. That made it sound as if she'd gotten that way by herself. Well, she hadn't. Like the old saying went, it took two.

He'd made Marissa pregnant. Pregnant! How in hell had he let such a thing happen? He'd been with a lot of women and he always used a condom unless it was a long-term relationship and he knew his lover well, knew she was using her own means of birth control. Things like that were just plain common sense.

Cullen took a long, cool mouthful of ale.

Where had his common sense gone that night? One look at Marissa and his hormones had sent his brain scuttling for shelter. That was no excuse, not unless you were seventeen and led around by your—

"...so the prince said, okay, O'Connell. You agree to one last hand. I'll put up my Maserati." Sean grinned. "Guess what I said?"

Cullen looked at his brother. He hadn't the foggiest notion what he was talking about. What now? Maybe a smile and a shrug of the shoulders would work.

"No idea," he said brightly.

Good choice. Sean nodded and began talking again. Cullen let his thoughts slip back to Marissa.

He'd never fallen into bed with a woman that fast, either. One minute he'd been reminding himself that he didn't think much of profs or alumni who got involved with grad students because it was far too easy for that kind of thing to happen and the next...

The next, she'd been in his arms.

Somewhere between the parking lot and his hotel room, he'd asked her if she was on the pill. Something like that, anyway; as he recalled, his brain cells had still been working then.

Yes, she'd said, and he'd thought, he'd thought...

He hadn't thought anything. He was too far gone. They both were, their mouths fused, their bodies on fire, his heart racing as he'd stripped off her clothes, tasted her sweetly rounded breasts, parted her golden thighs...

"Cull? You okay?"

Cullen blinked. Sean was watching him, pale blue eyes fixed on his face like lasers.

"Sure. I'm fine."

"Because for a second there, you looked—"

"I said I'm fine, kid." Cullen cleared his throat and made a show of peering around the restaurant. "Where's our waiter? We need another round."

Sean nodded. "Good idea."

"So," Cullen said brightly, "the prince bet his car, and—"

"What I said was, he *offered* to bet his car." Sean's gaze narrowed. "You haven't heard a thing I said, bro."

"Of course I did. This guy you were playing wanted to bet his, uh, his Porsche."

"It was a Maserati."

"Right. His Maserati. And you said—"

"And I said...?"

Great. They'd made this dinner appointment weeks before, when Sean phoned to say he'd be passing through Boston. Now, it was turning into a pop quiz.

He should have canceled it when he had the chance, but canceling would have raised a bucket of questions. Now it looked as if keeping the engagement was going to do the same thing.

"C'mon, man," Sean said lazily. "You get it right, I'll pick up the check. What did I say?"

Cullen flipped a mental coin and went for broke. "You said 'no.'"

"Like I said, you haven't been listening. You might as well be on another planet, for all the attention you're paying."

"My apologies. I didn't know your ego was on the line here."

"Take it easy, Cullen. Something's the matter. I want to know what it is."

"Nothing. Just some stuff at work..."

"Try again."

"What do I have to do? Go back to when we were kids, say 'Cross my heart, hope to die' before you believe me?"

"I wouldn't buy that, either. Face it, Cull. Bluffing doesn't work between us. I can read you like a book."

"Read this, then. Nothing's wrong."

"Right. That's why you came in here looking as if it was even money the world's going to end tomorrow morning."

Cullen gave a quick laugh. "Not that soon," he said, "but soon enough."

"If I have to, I'll put you in a hammerlock that'll wreck your shoulder for a week, same as when we were kids."

"Memory playing tricks on you, is it? It was the other way around."

Sean flashed a smile. "It was, until I stomped on your toe. Ma damn near murdered us both, remember? You limping, me cradling my arm... Cull. Talk to me, man. Whatever it is, it can't be that bad."

Cullen felt a muscle knot in his jaw. "Trust me," he said, after a few seconds, "it can."

"What'd you do?" Sean smiled again. "Don't tell me. You lost a case."

"I wish." Cullen took a deep breath, then raised his eyes to his brother's. "I made a woman pregnant."

Sean's face turned white. "What?"

Cullen stared at his brother. Then he swiveled around in his seat. "Damn it, where's that waiter?"

Without a word, Sean rose from the booth, marched to the bar in the front of the restaurant and returned two minutes later with a bottle of Wild Turkey and two glasses.

"They don't let you pour your own here," Cullen said aimlessly.

"They do now," Sean growled as he filled their glasses. He took a long swallow of his drink, then motioned to the one he'd put in front of Cullen. "Drink that. Then tell me I heard you right."

Cullen nodded and tossed down half his drink. He shuddered, wiped the back of his hand across his mouth and looked at his brother.

"A woman's carrying a baby, and I'm the man who did it."

"You're sure?"

Cullen nodded. "Yes."

"'Cause sometimes you can't be sure, you know? Just because a woman says—"

"I'm sure," Cullen said grimly. "You remember how Cassie looked the first few months she was pregnant? Pale, hollow-eyed, sick to her stomach in the mornings and exhausted all the rest of the day? Same symptoms here. Plus a belly that's gone from flat to—"

"For God's sake, I'm not asking if you're sure she's knocked up, I'm asking if you're sure the kid is yours."

"I'm almost positive."

"*Almost* positive? What's that supposed to mean? She tells you, 'I'm going to be a mama, and you're the papa,' and you believed her?"

"It wasn't like that."

"Did you do a paternity test?"

"Yes." Cullen remembered the look on Marissa's face when he'd demanded the test, how she'd said it wasn't necessary because she wanted absolutely nothing from him, how he'd said it wasn't up to her, nothing was up to her anymore. "I should have the results tomorrow."

"And then you'll know for sure?"

"Right. Then, I'll know."

"But for now, you assume you're the one who knocked the lady up because…?"

"Because I was there, and it happened."

Sean sat back. "When did she tell you?"

Cullen took a long swallow of bourbon. "Two weekends ago. Labor Day." He finished his bourbon and reached for the bottle. "Happy Labor Day," he said solemnly, "and isn't that one hell of a bad pun?"

"How'd it happen? Hell, don't laugh. You know what I mean."

"I wish I knew. I was—I was caught up in the moment."

"Too caught up to reach for a rubber?"

"Listen, kid, you asked me a question. You want an answer or not?" Cullen's mouth twisted. "I'm sorry. It was a reasonable thing to ask. I'm on edge, is all."

"She wasn't using anything? The pill?"

"She said she was, but she forgot she'd been off it for a few days… What?"

"Listen to yourself, Cullen. You were caught up in the moment. She said she was on the pill but she wasn't." Sean's eyes narrowed. "The lady sounds like she's running a scam on you."

Cullen felt his jaw tighten. "I don't think so."

"Well, I would. How long have you been sleeping with her?"

"I met her when I went out to Berkeley this past spring."

"And?"

"And what?"

"And, she's been seeing nobody but you all this time? She flies here, you fly there? You're the only guy who's been with her, what, the last three months?"

"Four months. We were only together that weekend. That night."

His brother's eyebrows rose. "You picked her up?"

"I didn't pick her up. She is—she *was* a third-year law student. My gofer for the weekend."

"Forgive me," Sean said sarcastically. "You *met* this babe—"

The knot in Cullen's jaw tightened again. "There's no need to refer to her that way."

He reached for the bottle of whiskey. Sean grabbed it first, capped it and shoved it aside.

"You don't need any more of this stuff. You're flying high without it. What's with you? You're the hot-shot attorney. Somebody in that fancy school you went to must have taught you how to recognize a scam when it comes up and bites you in the ass."

"You know what?" Cullen said softly. "I think we ought to end this discussion."

"Why? Don't you want to acknowledge the truth?" Sean leaned in, his eyes snapping with anger. "Face it. You met a clever babe, you fu—"

"Watch your mouth," Cullen said, his voice dangerously soft, his eyes suddenly cold.

Sean shook his head in disgust. "The lady's good, I'll give her that. She sure as hell must have screwed your brains out because now she says you knocked her up and—"

Cullen grabbed his brother by the front of his shirt and half-dragged him across the table.

"I told you to watch your mouth. You need me to back that up with something more than words?"

"Let go," Sean said quietly. "Or we're both going to regret what happens next."

The brothers stared at each other, the silence broken only by the rasp of their breaths. Then Cullen let go and sat back.

"Hell," he muttered. "I'm sorry."

"It's okay."

"It's just…Marissa wasn't even going to tell me what

had happened. If I hadn't looked her up…'' Cullen shook his head. "I don't understand the woman. She has no money, she had to quit school, she's working her tail off at a restaurant that looks like a health inspector's nightmare, she moved into a place gave me the creeps just to look at, and she insists she doesn't want anything from me.''

"Maybe. Maybe not. Maybe she's just smart enough to figure she's better off playing it that way." Sean's mouth thinned. "Go on, get that look on your face again. I don't give a damn. I just want to be sure you know what might be coming down before it's too late." He paused. "I take it the lady's going through with the pregnancy."

"Yes.''

"And what about you? Assuming it's yours, is that what you want? A kid walking around, carrying your genes?''

"You mean, would I want her to—'' Cullen's mouth tightened. "Hell, no. It's one thing to talk about things in the abstract. I'm still all for choice, but this is different. Besides, the decision's not really mine to make." He fell silent, stared into his empty glass and then raised his eyes to Sean's. "I always figured, another few years, I'd find the right woman, settle down, have a family…''

"And now?''

"And now… Well, if the child is mine—''

"I'm relieved to hear you say 'if.'''

"If it is, I'll do the right thing.''

"Meaning?''

"I'll pay for its support. And for Marissa's.''

Sean let out a long breath. "Thank God for small favors. For a second there, I thought you were saying you'd marry this woman.''

"Marry her? No way. We hardly know each other. I live here, she lives there. Why would I marry her?''

"Who knows? An overdeveloped sense of morality, maybe. Concern for how she'd raise the kid." Sean grinned in an attempt to ease the tension. "I'm glad to know you're not really crazy. It's one thing to take responsibility for your actions and another to jump into the deep end of the pool."

"Meaning?"

"Meaning, you can accept responsibility for paternity, if the test proves positive, without becoming a husband and father."

"No," Cullen said, "there's no danger of me doing that."

Sean heaved a sigh of relief. "I'm glad to hear it. Keep me posted, okay? And if you need a sounding board…"

"I'll call you."

A moment passed. Then Sean cleared his throat. "Hey," he said briskly, "did I tell you about this Swedish blonde I met in Monte Carlo?"

Cullen grinned. "How come they're always Scandinavian blondes?"

"What can I tell you? A man's got to adhere to a standard."

The brothers laughed and this time, when Sean told his story, Cullen did his best to pay attention. Even so, his thoughts kept wandering to what Sean had said about his taking responsibility without becoming a husband and father.

Court-ordered or self-imposed, responsibility without emotional involvement was the usual outcome of situations like the one Cullen was in.

The part of him that was a coolheaded lawyer had already started laying the foundation for such a plan. He would have his name on the child's birth certificate. He'd arrange for money to cover not just basic expenses but those that would ensure the child a good life.

There was only one problem.

Sean had said he could do the right thing without becoming a husband and father, but Sean was wrong. Wrong about part of it, anyway.

Cullen couldn't avoid being a father.

The day he'd planted his seed in Marissa's womb, a father was precisely what he'd become.

MARISSA shut the door of her apartment on the FedEx man, leaned back against it and stared at the envelope he'd just delivered.

She'd have known what it contained even if the return address hadn't said Bio Tech Labs in big blue and red letters. Nobody sent her official-looking packages. Not since she'd withdrawn from the university and surrendered the scholarship that had paid her room, board and tuition.

She swallowed past the lump in her throat. Here it was. The DNA-based paternity test report. Why was she so nervous? She knew what it would say.

Yes, but now Cullen would know it, too. He hadn't believed her when she'd told him he'd fathered her baby. Not that she could really blame him. Why would a man accept the word of a woman who fell into bed with him without knowing much more than his name?

Still, she couldn't come up with a reason why it should have mattered to him. He owed her nothing; she'd made that clear once he'd recovered from the shock of learning what their—their encounter had achieved. She *wanted* nothing. She'd made that clear, too.

"I assume you intend to go through with the pregnancy," he'd said.

She'd looked at him as if he were crazy. Did he think she'd given up everything she'd worked so hard for so she could get rid of the baby in her womb?

"Yes," she'd said calmly, "I do."

That was when he'd told her he'd want to see proof of his paternity.

"What for?" she'd said, and he'd looked at her as if this time she were the crazy one.

"So I can make the appropriate arrangements," he'd told her.

Marissa crossed the tiny living room, into the kitchen,

put the unopened envelope on the table and filled a kettle with water.

That was when she'd realized he intended to do something about his role in what had happened. Write her a check, ask her in turn to sign a document releasing him from all future obligation.

She put the kettle on the stove, turned on the burner and wondered if that put her a step ahead of her mother. Yes, she thought bitterly, it probably did. Cullen would at least acknowledge his participation in the creation of her child. Her son—she knew it was a boy, thanks to last week's amniocentesis that had also provided the DNA for Bio Tech Labs to sequence—her son wouldn't have a real father any more than she'd had, but at least she could tell him, when he was old enough, that his biological father had tried to do the right thing.

Not that she'd accept his help.

She wasn't going to do anything as demeaning as sign a paper like the one Cullen would undoubtedly produce. She didn't want anything from him. It was his problem if he couldn't accept that as the truth. She had a paycheck again—it had taken a couple of days, but Tony had finally agreed to let her come back. Even if he hadn't, she would never take a penny from Cullen.

Signing away her child's right to know his father, accepting money for such an agreement, would only make her feel dirtier than she already did.

"About me, baby," Marissa said softly, touching her palm lightly to her belly, "not about you."

Never that. From the moment she'd made the decision to go through with her pregnancy, she'd felt a connection to her child. Her son, she thought, and smiled. She would love him as she had not been loved, do whatever it took to make his life a happy one—

The kettle shrilled. At least, she thought it did but when she looked at it, it wasn't even steaming.

The doorbell.

That was a surprise. First the FedEx man and now, who? The superintendent, come to fix the toilet tank that had been running for days? Her downstairs neighbor, come to complain about the noise the continual flow of water was causing?

Marissa sighed, smoothed back her hair, undid all the locks but the chain, opened the door a crack…and felt her heart skid into her throat.

"Cullen?"

What a stupid question. Of course it was Cullen. You couldn't mistake him for anybody else. His height. His wide shoulders. Those deep blue eyes.

That hard, narrowed mouth that had once touched hers with such incredible passion…

"What are you doing here, Cullen?"

"Open the door, Marissa."

"We said all we needed to say last time."

"You want to discuss the child you're carrying through the door, that's fine. Why don't you give me a minute so I can ring your neighbor's bell? I'm sure she doesn't want to miss any of this."

Marissa tore off the chain and flung the door open. Cullen brushed past her. He was dressed formally, in a gray suit, white shirt and navy tie, and he was carrying a sleek leather briefcase.

The attorney, properly attired to do the bidding of his client, she thought bitterly, and lifted her chin.

"You're wrong, Cullen. We don't have anything to discuss."

"Shut the door."

Eyes flashing, she closed it with a bang. "Any other orders?"

"We *do* have things to talk about, Marissa. Private things that don't concern anyone but us."

Us. There was no "us." Just for a moment, weeks ago, when she'd first realized she was pregnant, she'd let herself dream of an "us"….

The kettle shrieked. Marissa spun toward the kitchen. She heard his footsteps following her across the worn linoleum. She didn't want to look at him, didn't want to see his face when he offered her money, and she bought time by busying herself with taking down a mug, putting a tea bag in it and filling it with water. When she finally turned around, Cullen was looking at the unopened envelope on the table.

"I see you got the DNA report."

She shrugged.

His eyes met hers. "You haven't opened it."

"I don't have to. I already know what it says."

"And now, thanks to a call to the lab, so do I."

"Surprised?" she said, trying for a cool tone but managing instead, she realized with dismay, to sound tremulous. "Did you actually think I'd lie about something like this?"

"I'm a partner in a large law firm," he said quietly. "I've seen a lot of things I wouldn't have believed."

He was right. She knew it. After a second, she drew a long breath, then let it out.

"Why have you come here?"

Cullen pulled a chair out from the table. "Sit down."

Her home, such as it was, and he was inviting her to sit down. Marissa lifted her chin.

"I'd rather stand, thank you."

"This is going to take a while," he said, and put the briefcase on the table where it looked incongruous enough to almost merit laughter, the softly expensive black leather lying on the scarred pine wood.

"I don't think so." Marissa put down the mug of tea and stuffed her hands into the pockets of her sweatpants. They were almost the only things she still owned that fit her. "Actually, I know why you've come."

His eyebrows rose. "You do?"

"Yes." She cleared her throat. Why did this feel so much like moot court? How could you sleep with a man, hold nothing back when he made love to you, and end up standing in a kitchen facing him as if you were not just strangers but adversaries? "Yes, I do. You want to do what you believe is the right thing."

A muscle knotted in his cheek. "Yes. I do."

"So you're going to offer me money."

Cullen folded his arms. "Go on."

"And you're going to ask me to sign documents that say I've accepted such and such a sum, blah blah blah, for which I release you from all future obligation, blah blah blah."

"That's a lot of blah," he said.

He made it sound like a small joke but it wasn't, not with that streak of ice in his tone. A feeling of apprehension tiptoed down her spine like the cold footprints of some tiny animal, but she wouldn't let that stop her. She was only a year away from her law degree and then she'd be qualified to take the Bar exam. Did he think she wouldn't have figured all this out without his sitting her down and explaining it to her?

"Of course," she said coolly, "you and I both know that anything I sign isn't worth the paper it's printed on."

"That's correct."

"I could go to a judge virtually anytime and tell him I'd made a mistake, settling for whatever you're going to offer me. That I needed more money, or that I hadn't had adequate representation."

"Correct again."

Marissa narrowed her eyes. "I'm telling you all this so you won't be too distressed when I also tell you I'm not going to sign anything."

"Indeed," he said. Actually, he almost purred it. Again, she felt that a sense of disquiet. Silly, to feel it. What could he do but accept her decision?

"I'm also not going to accept anything you've come to give me, Cullen. I told you, I don't want anything from you."

"What about my name on my son's birth certificate? Do you want that?"

She stared at him. What had happened to his references to "the child"? When had this baby become Cullen O'Connell's son?

"Answer me," he said sharply, taking a step toward her. "You have all these plans, Marissa. Where do my wishes fit in?"

"I—I'll name you on the birth certificate, if that's what you want. There's no reason for my baby to be a—a—"

"Bastard," Cullen said coldly. "That's the word you're looking for. There's no reason for him to be raised in poverty, either."

"Poverty isn't a disease!"

"Don't you think this child deserves a good start in life? Good schools? A home that isn't located in a war zone? Do you think he should grow up with a mother who's working in a dive and still can hardly make ends meet? I'm assuming you managed to get back your career-building job at the Chiliburger."

He smiled thinly; it reminded her of a wolf's snarl. She knew better than to tell him he was right.

"I have a plan," she said stiffly.

"Really."

He was mocking her. She knew she should ignore it, that he could wound only her pride, but pride was all she had left.

"I won't wait tables forever. Once I get on my feet financially, I'm going to finish the credits for my degree."

"And when will that happen? Five years from now? Ten?"

"What matters is that it will happen."

"Oh, sure," he said coldly. "But until then, what's going to happen to my son?"

"You keep saying that as if my baby belongs to you."

Again, that thin, wolfish smile. Cullen moved quickly; the next thing she knew he was holding her wrist clamped behind her back. "That baby belongs to me as much as he does to you."

"No! He doesn't! Damn you, Cullen—"

"Why do you hate me? You're pregnant, but that's your doing as much as mine."

"Let go. Let go!"

"You sure as hell didn't hate me the night we made love."

"It wasn't love. It was—it was immoral. It was wrong. It was—"

"It was what we both wanted, and you know it."

She tried to turn her face away from his, away from the icy glare of his angry eyes, and he clasped her chin and forced her to look at him.

"You burned for me that night, Marissa. You couldn't get enough of my hands on you, my mouth on you—"

Marissa spat a Spanish word at him. Cullen knew what it meant. Like his brothers, he'd dealt with Mexican workers on the grounds of the Desert Song in Las Vegas. They'd taught him their language, the best and the worst of it, and what she'd said was surely the worst.

"Liar," he said roughly, and he caught her mouth with his.

She fought him again, as hard as she had the last time. Sank her teeth into his lip, beat against his chest, but he went on kissing her, kissing her…

And felt the instant of her surrender. Her mouth softened under his; her sigh whispered against his lips.

Now, his fevered body told him. Lift her in your arms, take her to the bedroom, bury yourself in her again as you did that first time…

Cullen jerked back.

His hand fell to his side; he dragged air into his burning lungs and watched as Marissa's eyes flew open, as she staggered back against the table. They stared at each other in the taut silence of the hot afternoon and then she swung away from him.

"All right." Her voice was a croak. "Give me whatever you want me to sign. I'll take the check, too, just so you can have a clear conscience, but I promise you, I'll rip it in half just as soon as—"

"No."

Cullen's voice was like the snap of a whip. Marissa turned and stared at him.

"But you said—"

"*You* said. Never tell a man you know what he said before he says it. Nine times out of ten, you'll be wrong— and the tenth time, he'll do just the opposite to spite you."

She watched him, her eyes searching his for a hint of the true meaning of his words. Something awful, she knew; she could feel it in her bones.

"Then, why did you come here today?"

He smiled, and she knew she would remember the chill of that smile forever.

"I came to tell you what happens next," he said softly.

"What—what happens next?"

Cullen nodded. He'd thought about this a thousand times after his dinner with Sean, gone through the plan, gone over it, refined it...

And finally admitted that what he and Sean had agreed upon wasn't the right solution.

Like it or not, the child growing in Marissa Perez's womb was his.

Like it or not, he was responsible not just for its conception but for its life.

Like it or not, by late last night, he could think of only one appropriate plan of action.

"What happens next," he said slowly, his eyes on Marissa's face, "is that you're going to become my wife."

CHAPTER SIX

CULLEN was asking her to be his wife.

His wife!

Was he really suggesting she marry him? It was so preposterous she wanted to laugh…but the hardness in his eyes made it clear he wasn't joking.

"Well?" he said. "No reaction? That's not like you, Marissa. You always have something to say."

He was so smug. So sure of himself. Did he expect her to drop at his feet in gratitude? Was she supposed to applaud his sacrifice? Tie herself to a man who didn't want her, so he could salve his conscience?

He was in for the shock of his life.

She smiled. Casually, even graciously, as if she'd expected his proposal all along.

"Thank you," she said politely. "But I'm not interested."

"Not interested." His smile thinned. "*You're* not interested."

"That's right. It's a generous offer, but—"

"It's not generous, and it's not an offer. It's a logical argument for marriage. My son isn't going to be born a bastard."

She knew he was using the word to intimidate her, but she wasn't about to be intimidated. She could, and would, stand up to the Cullen O'Connells of this world.

"That's an outdated concept," she said calmly.

"In your world, perhaps. Not in mine."

"Ah. Yes, of course. That rarified air you breathe makes

everything different. I keep forgetting that. I already said I'll put your name on his birth certificate since it means so much to you.''

''Since it means so much to me?'' Cullen narrowed his eyes. ''What about what it'll mean to my son, when he's old enough to ask questions? Don't you think he'd want to know his father's name?''

He was right. Why not admit it? But before she could, Cullen was lecturing her again.

''Didn't it occur to you he'd have questions when he's older? What did you intend to tell him, when he began asking about his father?''

What, indeed? She'd been so busy thinking about how to get through the next months, she hadn't had time to think about what would happen years down the road. All she knew was that she wouldn't repeat her mother's endless litany of anger and accusation.

''I didn't think about—''

''No,'' Cullen snapped. ''I'm sure you didn't''

''I'll tell him something,'' Marissa said stubbornly. ''There's plenty of time to decide.''

Cullen's eyes locked on hers. ''You won't have to make those decisions because he won't ask those questions. He'll know I'm his father, right from the start.''

''You can't be serious about marriage. We don't know anything about each other.''

''We knew enough about each other to make a child. Remember?''

Remember? Sometimes she lay awake nights, wondering if she'd ever be able to forget.

''Children aren't stupid, Cullen. My son—''

''Our son,'' he said coldly.

''The point is, it will only confuse him if you pop in and out of his life. I know you think you want that now, but given time—''

''Did I say anything about popping in and out of his life?''

"Surely you weren't talking about a real marriage."

"Two people living together. Having dinner at the same table at night. Raising their child together. If that's what you mean by a real marriage, you're damned right it's what I'm talking about."

"It wouldn't work. How could it?" she said desperately. "I don't want—"

"I don't give a damn what you want. I'm talking about doing what's best for our child."

Cullen swung away, shrugged off his jacket and tossed it on the back of a chair, followed that by undoing his tie, his shirt collar and his cuffs. She knew her horrid box of an apartment was hot as the anteroom to Hades, but even in her anger, seeing the strong, tanned column of his throat and his hair-dusted, well-muscled forearms made her remember things she didn't want to remember.

Marissa turned her back, dumped her mug in the sink and walked into the living room. It was, if anything, hotter than the kitchen and the mismatched old furniture made it feel like a trap.

Cullen had followed her in and she could feel his presence behind her. Big. Commanding. Almost overwhelming, and she let herself imagine, just for a moment, what it would be like to be his wife, before she turned and confronted him.

"Look," she said briskly, "I appreciate what you're trying to do, but it's not necessary."

"I don't think you have any idea what it is I'm *going* to do, Marissa."

She caught the difference between his choice of words and hers. Ignore it, she told herself fiercely. He was just trying to shake her.

"Cullen. Really, I don't—"

"This isn't about you." His tone was whip-sharp. "It's not about me. It's about our child."

He put his hand over her belly. She caught her breath,

stunned at the image of Cullen cradling the small, helpless life inside her that flashed into her mind.

"There's not a way in the world," he said, "I'd let my son be raised like this."

"Like what?" Marissa moved away from his touch, struggling for composure. "Are you telling me I'm not fit to raise my own child?"

"Our child. And I'm not talking about your fitness to be a parent, I'm talking about the kind of life you can afford to give him."

"He'll have the best I can manage. Poverty doesn't necessarily limit someone," she said, trying not to wince at the absolute hypocrisy of her own words. It was true that poverty didn't have to limit your dreams, but the truth was that being poor was horrible. Only a fool would deliberately choose such a life.

Why was she saying these things? In her heart, she knew Cullen was doing the right thing. He wanted to accept full responsibility for his child. How could she fault that? How could she turn it down? *Why* was she turning it down?

Why? Because she'd gotten herself into this mess. She didn't need anyone to get her out of it. She didn't need Cullen O'Connell, didn't want him...

Liar, a voice inside her whispered slyly. *Liar, liar, liar!*

Her body flushed with heat; her eyes met Cullen's. He was watching her as if he knew what was going through her mind. She let out a shaky breath and turned away. She had to get him out of here before she said something, did something, she'd regret.

"Thank you for your offer," she said politely, "but marrying you is out of the question. We have nothing more to discuss. Please do us both a favor and go away."

"You'd like that, wouldn't you?" Cullen grabbed her shoulder. "If I just got out of your life? If you could pretend you'd never slept with me?"

Marissa gave a bitter laugh. "It's too late for that."

"Yes. It is," Cullen said through his teeth. "But it's not too late for some answers."

"You've had all the answers I'm going to give. I don't want to marry you. That's the end of it."

"Like hell it is!" He spun her toward him, his face dark with anger. "Why didn't you call and tell me you were pregnant?"

"What a good idea," she said coldly. "I can hear the conversation now. 'Hi. This is Marissa Perez. Remember me? I'm the woman you—'"

"Don't give me that crap. You knew I'd remember you. I phoned you a dozen times after that weekend and you never returned my calls."

"I lead a busy life. That's why I have an answering machine."

"Oh, right. You have an answering machine." A thin sneer curved Cullen's mouth. "Do you ever bother checking it for messages?"

Marissa stared at him. What would he say if he knew she'd listened to his messages over and over? That there'd been times she'd played them just to hear his voice?

But she'd known what he wanted, why he'd he called. She wasn't stupid.

She'd been pathetically easy.

Living with that knowledge was bad enough; phoning him, letting him know she hadn't forgotten him, would have been worse. Flying across the country for the weekend was nothing to a man like him. He'd have come to see her, she'd have tumbled into bed with him again and lost what little self-respect she had left.

The only humiliation greater than that would have been calling to tell him she was pregnant.

"Well? I'm still waiting for you to tell me why you didn't answer my calls."

"Wrong," she said. "You asked me to explain why I didn't tell you I was pregnant. Just for the sake of argument, let's suppose I had. What would you have said to me?''

''The same thing I'm saying now. That this child is as much my responsibility as yours.''

''Aren't you leaving something out?'' She heard the tremor in her voice and vowed she wouldn't let him see her weep. ''First you'd have said, 'Pregnant, Marissa? Why tell me? Who else have you been with?' And then you'd have demanded a DNA test.''

Cullen's eyes narrowed. ''You're damned right, I would. A woman tells a man she's been with once that she's having his child and he's not supposed to ask questions?''

No, she thought, *oh no, because if the night meant as much to you as it did to me...*

The thought, its implications, turned her legs to water. She jerked free of his hands and sat down in a straight-backed chair near the window.

''All right,'' she said calmly, ''I'm willing to admit you have the right to some interest in my baby.''

Cullen smiled tightly. ''How generous.''

''And that he can benefit from some connection with his father.''

''Another crumb. Go on.''

Marissa knotted her hands together in her lap. ''I'm willing to acknowledge you as my child's father. But I don't want your money. And I certainly don't want some—some sham marriage to assuage your guilt.''

''Is that what you think this is all about? Guilt?''

''No,'' she said sweetly, ''of course not. I think you just suddenly developed a desperate yearning for fatherhood.'' She sprang to her feet. ''Of course it's guilt,'' she snapped. ''What else would you call it?''

''Responsibility,'' he said coldly. ''For my actions. Or is that a concept that's beyond your comprehension?''

She wanted to laugh. To cry. To ball up her fist and hit him for his insufferable arrogance. She looked around at the awful place she'd taken to save money for her baby and finally permitted herself a bark of joyless laughter.

"When I found out I was pregnant," she said, "I considered my options. Abortion. Adoption. The intelligent, responsible solutions that sound so wise until you find yourself with a life inside you. And I knew that neither was the right choice for me."

"Ah." Cullen's voice was even more frigid. "So you decided on martyrdom instead."

"You son of a bitch! Is that what you think? That I gave everything for some—some misbegotten martyr's complex?" Her voice broke. Angry tears burned her eyes and she turned away. "Go home, Cullen," she whispered. "You've done your bit. Now, please, just go away."

There was a long silence. She heard his footsteps behind her, felt the light pressure of his hands on her shoulders. He tried to turn her to him but Marissa stood fast.

"You love this baby," Cullen said quietly.

She didn't answer. She didn't have to. Her answer was visible in the sacrifices she'd willingly made so she could keep the child. Why hadn't he understood that until now?

"Marissa. If you love him," he said quietly, "then you must want the best for him. So do I. A good home. Good schools. Most of all, two parents who'll be there for him. Are those such terrible things to want a kid to have?" Gently, inexorably, he turned her to face him. Her eyes were shiny with tears and he felt something tight start to unknot inside him. "Marriage is the right thing. In your heart, you know that's true."

"It wouldn't work."

"Why not?"

"Because—because, how could it?"

He smiled. It was such an illogical answer from a woman he knew prided herself for her logic.

"We'd make it work. We're two intelligent people. We'll find a way."

She shook her head. "We're strangers."

"No. We spent a night together." His voice dropped to a husky whisper. He hadn't meant to remind her of that but holding her like this, his fingers spread over the delicate bones in her shoulders, her face turned up to his, her eyes full of questions, Cullen felt the memory sweep over him. His gaze dropped to her mouth. "A night I've never forgotten."

Color striped her cheeks. "You can't possibly think sex is enough to build a marriage on," she whispered.

"Marriages have been built on less."

"Yes, but—"

There was only one way to silence her, and Cullen took it. He trapped her face in his hands and took her mouth with his. She made a little sound of surprise and tried to pull back; he took her bottom lip between his teeth and nipped the full, sweet flesh. God, the taste of her. Strawberries, he thought, sweet summer strawberries on a sun-drenched hill, and as he thought it, Marissa whimpered, leaned into him and opened her mouth to his. Cullen groaned, gathered her tight in his arms and kissed her with all the pent-up hunger of the last months.

She whispered a soft word in Spanish, moved closer, moved against him. She felt soft. Warm. Incredibly female, her breasts and body lush as they prepared for the birth of his child.

Mine, he thought fiercely. *All of this, mine.*

An eternity passed before Cullen lifted his head. When he did, Marissa was trembling in his arms, her breathing ragged. She looked small and shaken and all he wanted was to draw her to him again and comfort her.

"Marissa." He ran his hand along the side of her face, threaded his fingers into her silky curls and stroked them back from her flushed cheek. "How long will it take you to pack?"

"Pack?"

"Your things. Whatever you can't part with. Leave everything else and we'll buy whatever you want in Boston."

She stiffened in his embrace, put her hands against his chest. He didn't want to, but he dropped his arms to his sides.

"I'm not marrying you. I keep telling you that. Why won't you listen? I don't need your help. I don't need anyone's help." She stepped back and stood facing him, small white teeth bared like those of a cornered animal. "Go away, Cullen. You offered what you saw as the right thing and I turned you down. Surely, that's enough to make you feel good about yourself."

"You have a hell of a poor opinion of me."

"I don't have any opinion of you. I just want you to leave."

Cullen walked to the sofa, opened his briefcase and took out what she recognized as a legal document.

"Here," he said, and thrust it at her.

She took the paper from him but her gaze never left his. "What is it?"

"You're a third-year law student. Read it and find out."

She didn't move, didn't stop looking at him while the silence and the heat built in the small room. At last, she started reading.

He watched her, saw her face begin to drain of color. After a couple of minutes, Cullen walked to the window, drew up a shade so ancient it threatened to disintegrate in his hands and looked out on the street.

How would she react to what he'd handed her? With relief, a cold voice inside him said. With outrage, another voice whispered.

Truth was, he didn't know. She'd made an impassioned speech about wanting her baby but predicting her reactions to anything was turning out to be as impossible as predicting the ultimate path of a tornado.

After his talk with Sean the other night, he'd drafted the documents that would ensure a monthly stipend for the child in Marissa's womb, straight through to a university degree. As Sean had pointed out, that was all that was required of him ethically. Hell, it was more, considering the amount of money he'd decided to provide.

Except, that simple word—*father*—kept haunting him. He was going to be a father. He hadn't planned it, hadn't wanted it, not now. Someday in the future, sure. That's what a man did, wasn't it? Find the right woman, settle down to a pleasant if uneventful married life, have kids…

Fate, and one night of unthinking passion, had changed all that.

A tiny life floated serenely in Marissa's womb. A life he'd sired, and even though the timetable was off, that newcomer deserved all the things Cullen had intended a child of his would have. The things he'd told Marissa. A good home and good schools. Two parents. And other things almost as important. A dog. A cat. A tank full of guppies, if that was what the kid wanted. Electric trains and a bike, and Christmas mornings filled with joy.

Most of all, his child would have what Cullen had never had. A father who loved him enough to put him first and to put everything else, including his own pleasures, second.

It was the right way. The only way. Once he'd admitted that, he'd known that putting his name on a birth certificate and funding a bank account would never be sufficient.

Late last night, he'd drawn up a new document. Even then, he hadn't really been sure he'd use it. At dawn, exhausted, he'd tucked both sets of papers into his briefcase and stumbled to bed, telling himself he'd make his choice on the flight to California.

Instead, he'd made it only moments ago. For better or for worse, what he'd handed Marissa was a prenuptial agreement.

Cullen looked at her. She was still reading the document but he knew she was almost at the end by the look on her face. Well, he hadn't expected her to be thrilled by all it spelled out. He'd set out her choices. It was up to her to react to them.

Marissa looked up. The document he'd drafted hung limply from her hand.

"This is a contract," she said slowly.

"All those classes on contract law weren't wasted, were they?"

"Don't joke with me, damn it! You've drawn up a prenup!"

"Exactly."

"Marriage," she said, spitting out the word like an obscenity.

"Marriage," he said calmly. "That's what I've been talking about for the past hour."

"Forget it!" She stepped away from him, her color high. "Here's what I've been telling *you* for the last hour, Mr. O'Connell. I will not marry you. Never. Do you understand? As for the rest of this—this piece of garbage…" Eyes locked to his, she tore the document he'd given her in half, then in half again. The ripped paper fluttered to the worn carpet like white ribbons. "You know what you can do with it."

"Did you read it carefully?"

"You mean, the part that says we'll review the situation every two years?" Marissa laughed. "A loophole so you can institute divorce proceedings, when you've had enough."

"I'm not planning on divorce, Marissa. It's simply a safeguard for us both."

"It's an admission this will never work."

"I'm not going to argue the point," Cullen said calmly. "Besides, I was referring to the clause that sets out my financial commitment to you. It says—"

"I know what it says. You'll provide me with…what was the phrase? 'The appropriate financial support due a spouse.'"

Cullen felt his face heat. The words had a nasty sound, stated so baldly.

"It also says," he said quickly, "that I'll pay your tuition at Harvard Law."

"Just think," Marissa said coolly. "All I cost you that night we went to bed was dinner. Heck, not even that. The law club picked up the tab."

"Damn it," Cullen snarled, closing the distance between them, clasping her elbows and hoisting her to her toes. "What's the matter with you?"

"What's the matter with *you?*" she shot back. "Do you think I'm still the same silly girl who foolishly tumbled into bed that night with you?"

"We made love that night. And we made a baby. There's nothing foolish in that."

No, she thought, there wasn't. Creating a life was serious business.

"What am I asking that's so impossible, Marissa? I want you to marry me. Be my wife. Help me make things right for our son."

Oh, how easy he made it all sound! Marriage, and a perfect life for their baby...

"We already agreed, we'd start ahead of some couples."

She hadn't agreed to anything, but that didn't seem to matter, especially when she knew, in her heart, her case was weak. What kind of woman would deny her baby the advantages Cullen was offering?

"Other people aren't strangers," she said wearily. "They have shared hopes and concerns."

"We have shared hopes and concerns."

She laughed, or tried to. "Sure we do. I'll bet you're always hoping you'll be able to pay the rent when it comes due, and concerned what will happen if you don't."

"You're proving my point about the logic of marrying me," Cullen said quietly, "but that's not what I mean. I'm talking about things that matter. Like our love for the law. And I'll bet we share an interest in more than that."

"For instance."

He thought for a minute. "Music."

"I like Mozart."

He sighed. "I like stuff that came a little later."

"How much later?"

"Say..." A little smile flickered at the corners of his mouth. "Say, the late 1970s?"

Upset as she was, it was hard not to smile, too, but she didn't. Instead, she shook her head.

"Look, Cullen, I know you mean well, but—"

"How about boats? Do you like to sail?"

"As in, on the water?"

Cullen laughed. "Yeah. As in, on the water."

Marissa shuddered. "More water than can fit in a bathtub makes me nervous. Face it, okay? We come from different worlds. Even if—*if*, mind you, I were to consider marr—"

"Don't consider it," he said gruffly. "Just do it."

She started to speak but he stopped her with a gentle kiss, a soft brush of his lips against hers. Maybe it was that gentleness that was her undoing. There'd been so little that was gentle in her life...

"Marissa," Cullen whispered, and she let herself sink into the kiss. Into the hard comfort of his body, the warmth of his encircling arms, let herself imagine having this man, this strong, determined, sexy man, to lean on.

The thought dazzled her. Frightened her. She'd never lean on anybody, or be foolish enough to put her trust in a man.

"You see?" Cullen said huskily. "We can make this work."

"With sex, you mean. But—"

"But what?" He cupped her face and his eyes blazed into hers. "Is it wrong for a man to want his wife in his bed?"

"Yes. When they don't know each other. When their marriage is an expedient mockery. When—when they should never have—"

He kissed her again, harder this time, and as the kiss deepened, the earth seemed to drop out from beneath her.

Marissa moaned and clung to Cullen's shoulders. Wrong, she thought dizzily, oh, this was wrong. She was giving in to a base need again, admitting to the terrifying emotions that could only be her undoing.

"Cullen," she gasped, "Cullen, I think—"

"Stop thinking," he said fiercely. "Just feel. Just do it. Marry me."

How could she? And yet, how could she not? All this time that she'd been telling Cullen he was crazy to even suggest marriage, she knew she was being selfish. She had a child to think of. A life dependent on her that hadn't asked to come into this world.

"If I did," she heard herself say, "if I did, you'd have to agree to no sex."

"And give up the only thing besides the law that we have in common?"

He said it seriously but she knew he was laughing at her, and it made her all the more determined. Her breathing quickened. She'd always been good at chess. Wasn't that what this was? A game of chess...and she'd just check-mated him. She'd given Cullen a reason to withdraw his marriage offer. Surely, he was too virile a man to accept a sexless marriage.

"I can see right through you," he said softly.

"Excuse me?"

"You tie on a stipulation you assume I won't accept, and the onus is off you. We don't get married, but it's my doing, not yours."

Her laugh sounded false even to her own ears. "That's nonsense!"

"I don't think so. I think it's exactly what you're hoping will happen."

"Well, I don't care what you think." Marissa stepped out of his arms. "Your choice, Cullen. Take it or leave it."

Cullen narrowed his gaze on Marissa's determined, lovely face. He thought about telling her there wasn't a way in hell he'd accept her terms for very long, or pointing out that she was kidding herself if she thought she could live with them, either. For reasons that were beyond him, she couldn't seem to accept the truth, that she was the most sensual, sexual woman he'd ever known.

"Well?" she said. "What's your answer?"

He gave her a smile she couldn't read. Then he rolled his sleeves up another inch, took a quick look around him, and said she had better start packing.

Her heart thumped against her ribs. "Does that mean you accept my terms?"

"It means," he said calmly, "you have an hour before we walk out of this place and never come back to it."

"An hour? That's impossible."

"Nothing's impossible," he said, his eyes never leaving hers, "if you want it badly enough."

Were the softly spoken words a threat? Marissa couldn't tell, and she wasn't about to ask.

"Marissa?"

She looked up at him. A little smile curved his lips, but his eyes were cold. Whose chess game was in danger now, she wondered. His...or hers?

"An hour," she said briskly, and hoped he couldn't see that she was trembling as she went into the bedroom, opened the closet and took down her suitcase.

CHAPTER SEVEN

How could life get so complicated so fast? A man wanted to do what was right and ended up stepping into quicksand.

Two weeks had passed. Fourteen days. Three hundred and thirty-six hours. If you thought about it as blocks of time on a calendar, it wasn't much at all.

But when you'd lived through those hours, those days, those weeks, it was like viewing eternity from the inside out. How could time move so slowly?

Cullen stood on the terrace of his town house, overlooking the garden, a cup of coffee slowly going cold in his hand. Fall was trying to make a showing, but it wasn't succeeding. Though the leaves were starting to turn red and gold, the temperature was still as high as in midsummer.

That was too bad. He liked autumn. The brilliant blaze of foliage, the cool evenings... But this year's weather patterns seemed confused.

Like him.

Confused? No. Hell, no. He wasn't confused. Why would he be? Marissa despised him. She despised this place. She refused to speak to him, refused to look at him, refused, even, to acknowledge his presence.

There wasn't a damned thing confusing about that.

Cullen took a sip of coffee and made a face. The coffee was as cold as the mood inside the house but the coffee, at least, he could put aside.

Not so Marissa. She was his wife.

His untouched, unsmiling, Sphinx-silent wife.

Divorce would solve the problem. Half the people he

knew were divorced or separated. Giving up on marriage after only a couple of weeks wouldn't even make most of them blink. One of his firm's associates had just handled the breakup of a couple whose try at marital bliss had lasted exactly nine days.

Not that he'd expected bliss. He'd married for a purpose. Bliss had nothing to do with it. It was just that he'd had it with his wife treating him like he was a monster.

Even his housekeeper had taken to glaring at him. Concepcion came in at eight three mornings a week. As luck would have it, he'd had a deposition scheduled the day after Marissa's arrival, and God only knew how his Ice Bride had introduced herself.

Judging by the way Concepcion looked at him now, Marissa had probably told her she was being held captive in a modern-day version of Bluebeard's castle.

Was this what a man got for doing the right thing?

Cullen scowled, folded his arms and turned his back to the view.

He *had* done the right thing. That was one conviction that hadn't changed. So what if the woman who'd once looked at him with passion smoldering in her eyes now practically spat at him when their eyes met? What Marissa felt for him, what he felt for her, was secondary to the reason for their marriage—the child she carried.

His wife loathed him, Cullen thought grimly. Was it because he'd taken her out of her wonderful life in a Berkeley slum? Because she wasn't on her feet twelve hours a day in that ptomaine palace? Did she miss climbing four flights of stairs to a three-room sweatbox filled with furniture the Salvation Army would have rejected?

Oh yeah. He'd certainly given her reason to loathe him.

Add in law school, and anyone could see that he'd really treated her badly. If she ever got around to talking to him, he'd tell her he'd already done some checking. There was still time for her to apply to Harvard Law, but he'd be damned if he'd tell her that.

Let her approach him. Let her say something. Anything. Damn it, if she hated him, let her say so.

Let her say anything, he thought, and his scowl deepened.

The truth was, Marissa didn't talk, didn't look at him, didn't seem to be living on the same planet. As for emotion…the last time she'd shown him any was in her apartment. She'd stopped talking as soon as she'd agreed to become his wife. By the time they'd reached the airport, her sitting beside him like a mannequin in a wax museum, he'd started to wonder if doing the right thing was all it was cracked up to be.

That was why he'd decided to make a fast stop at Vegas, the center of quickie weddings, before heading for home. He'd intended to ask a judge he knew to tie the knot once they were in Boston, but Marissa's stony face, her expression of utter contempt had made him change his plans. Better to say "I do" in front of a stranger than an acquaintance who'd wonder what in hell was going on.

"You want any special kind of ceremony?" he'd asked Marissa at the airport.

No, she'd said. Just no. Not a smile, not a question, just that one cold word.

So he'd rented a car, driven down the Strip and pulled in at the first place he saw. The chapel had a ten-foot-tall statue of Elvis outside, complete with sideburns and blue suede shoes. Inside, the walls were covered with red satin hearts.

For one crazy minute, he'd considered turning around and dragging Marissa out of there, telling her nobody's marriage should start in a place as phony as this.

But sanity had prevailed, the same as when he'd thought about phoning the Desert Song and telling his mother he was in town. What would he have said? *Hi, Ma, guess what? I'm getting hitched and by the way, you'll be a grandma in five months?*

Right. That was just what a mother wanted to hear.

For now, Mary didn't know about Marissa. Nobody in his family did. Not yet. Well, Sean, but Sean didn't know the rest of it. That he was married...

Married. Was there a stranger-sounding word in the English language?

Standing in that red-silk chapel, facing a woman showing all the enthusiasm of a condemned prisoner on the gibbet, he'd ground his teeth together, barked out such a snappish "I do" that the J.P. had given him a look.

Marissa had whispered hers. That had really gotten the justice of the peace's attention.

"Are you all right, Ms. Perez?" he'd asked, his gaze dropping not so discreetly to Marissa's swollen belly.

"I'm fine," she'd replied. "Let's just get on with it, please."

The J.P. had made a joke of it after pronouncing them husband and wife.

"It's always nice to see a bride who's eager to tie the knot," he'd said.

Cullen had laughed politely, the J.P. had done the same, but Marissa had gone on looking like a corpse warmed over. In the end, nobody had fooled anybody. Marissa Perez had become Marissa O'Connell, and the occasion had not been a joyous one.

A muscle knotted in Cullen's jaw. He lifted the cup of coffee to his lips, grimaced and drank it down.

Did she think *he* was happy about this marriage? Oh, yeah. What man wouldn't be happy to have a wife who stayed in her rooms when he was around? Who refused to join him for meals? Who treated him as if she had never sighed in his arms, begged for his kisses, moaned his name when he spread her thighs and buried himself inside her?

The cup, squeezed far too tightly, shattered in Cullen's hand. He cursed, looked down at the white porcelain shards lying at his feet. Why was he thinking about the past? The future was all that mattered. The future, and the child in Marissa's womb.

Cullen slid open the terrace door, walked to the kitchen and took a dustpan and broom from the utility closet.

He was a civilized man, and his marriage was a civilized arrangement. That was what he'd promised himself during the long flight home from Nevada with Marissa never looking at him, never speaking a word, as if that swift flare of desire just a couple of hours before, in her apartment, had never happened.

It had infuriated him. What kind of game was she playing?

He'd made himself a vow.

He wouldn't touch her. He didn't want her in his bed if he had to battle past a show of contempt before he could get her to admit she wanted him. Sex had gotten them into this arrangement, but the well-being of a child was what would maintain it.

Out on the terrace again, Cullen was sweeping up the pieces of the cup when he noticed a smear of crimson on the broom handle and drops of crimson on the terrace floor. He'd gashed himself on the damned cup and never realized it. He headed back inside to get a bandage and saw that he'd left a trail of tiny blood drops across the pearl-gray Berber carpet.

That was all Concepcion needed. If he didn't get the mess cleaned up before she came back from the supermarket, she'd probably—

"You're bleeding!"

Cullen jerked around. Marissa was standing at the top of the wide marble step that led into the living room from the foyer. Her face was the same color as the marble.

"Marissa?"

She opened her mouth, shut it and swayed unsteadily on her feet. Cullen dropped the dustpan and broom and ran to her.

"Marissa," he said, scooping her into his arms, "what is it?"

"I'm all right," she whispered, but he could see that she wasn't.

"*¡Madre de Dios!* Is it the baby?"

Cullen looked up and saw Concepcion standing in the foyer, her black eyes wide with shock.

"I don't know. My wife just collapsed."

"I didn't collapse," Marissa said shakily. "Really. Just put me down. I'm fine."

Cullen and the housekeeper both ignored her.

"Sit the *señora* on the sofa. Put her head down. *Sí,* like that." Concepcion clasped her hands over her bosom. "She must be losing the child. The blood…"

"It's mine, not hers." Cullen squatted beside his wife and clasped her hands. "Marissa. Talk to me."

"I told you, I'm fine. I just felt dizzy for a minute."

"*¿Señora? ¿Se sucede qué? ¿Es el bebé?*"

Marissa shook her head. "*El bebé está muy bien. Acabo de sentirme mareado. La sangre…*"

"*Ah. Sí. La sangre.*"

Cullen's head swiveled from one woman to the other. How come it hadn't occurred to him that these two might share a language?

And how come Marissa had more of a relationship with his housekeeper than with him?

Damn it to hell, how come he didn't know the first thing about his own wife?

"What?" he demanded. "What's she saying?"

"It was the sight of the blood. It made her feel faint."

Cullen looked at his hand. The bleeding had stopped but there were spots on the carpet and there was some on his jeans. Based on how his housekeeper was glaring at him, she probably figured he'd taken to using small children and bunny rabbits for pagan sacrifice.

"It's nothing," he told Marissa, "just a little cut. A cut," he repeated, for the housekeeper's benefit.

Concepcion nodded. "I will take care of it."

"That's okay. I'll do it."

"I will do it, *señor.*"

"I said…" Hell. He sounded like a petulant ten year old. "Thank you, Concepcion. But for now, would you get us a cold compress?"

"I don't need one," Marissa said. She looked at him. "I'm fine. Really."

She didn't look fine, Cullen thought. She looked almost the way she had in Berkeley. Pale. Shadowed eyes. A mouth that trembled. Hadn't two weeks of rest and good nourishment done her any good?

"A cold compress will make you feel better."

She shook her head, sat up straight and carefully drew her hands from his. It didn't take a shrink to see that she was drawing back into herself.

She didn't want any help from anyone, especially him.

Concepcion clomped into the room with an ice pack, handed it to him and clomped out again to collect the fallen groceries. She disappeared into the kitchen and Marissa started to rise to her feet.

Cullen caught her hand and kept her beside him.

"Take it easy for a couple of minutes."

"I told you, I'm—"

"Fine. Right. Indulge me a little, okay? Let me put this ice pack on the back of your neck while you sit here."

He could tell that she was warring with herself. Should she leave to prove she didn't need to take his advice? A couple of seconds went by. Then she sighed, probably in resignation, and some of the rigidity ebbed from her posture.

"Give me the ice."

"I'll take care of it. You just lean forward. That's it."

She bent her head. Cullen swept her hair from the nape of her neck. The skin looked soft. Tender. He wondered what she'd do if he pressed his mouth to it instead of the ice.

"Ridiculous, isn't it?" she said. "A grown woman passing out at the sight of blood?"

He smiled, laid the ice pack gently against the exposed skin beneath her hair.

"We were on a picnic one time and a spider fell into my sister Megan's soup. She screeched like a banshee, her eyes rolled up into her head and she fell facedown into the bowl."

Marissa made a sound he figured someone would make when they tried not to laugh. "She must have been very young."

"She was twenty."

She did laugh this time. For some reason he couldn't fathom, that made him feel good.

"Okay, she was five. But it was a memorable performance." Cullen kept the ice in place and sat down on the step next to Marissa. "I'm sorry you had a scare." His mouth curved in a smile. "On the other hand, it was worth a little loss of blood to know you care."

"I don't…" Her cheeks reddened. "It had nothing to do with you."

"Ah. I should have known. I could have fallen at your feet, a Vorple blade in my heart, and you wouldn't have blinked."

She stared at him. "A Vorple what?"

"A Vorple blade." Cullen grinned and brandished an imaginary sword snatched from an imaginary scabbard at his hip. "Like Darth Vader's light saber, only ten times more deadly."

Marissa bit back another laugh. Laughing with this man would be a mistake. Anything that meant she was letting her guard down would be a mistake.

The entire flight to Boston two weeks ago, all she'd been able to think was that she was up in the air in more ways than one. Cullen O'Connell had come along, kicked the ground out from under her feet, forced her to admit that what he kept calling the right thing was exactly that.

And she was terrified.

Of course, she could never let him know that.

Was this how Dorothy had felt, swept up by that Kansas tornado and dropped down in the land of Oz? This absolute disorientation? This dizzying sense of fear? Except, in the mythical land of Oz, Dorothy had a tin man, a scarecrow and a lion to comfort her.

Marissa had nobody. Nobody but the man sitting next to her right now, his thigh brushing hers, his hand enfolding hers…

But she didn't have him. He'd done his duty, as he saw it. Married her. Brought her east. Installed her in his home…

In a guest room in his home.

Separate rooms. Separate lives. He'd rushed off the very first morning she was here, left her a stiffly worded note about having a deposition, as if he'd needed an excuse to explain what she'd understood all along.

She was his wife, but she wasn't ever going to be part of his life. And that was fine. That was how she wanted it. It was the only way she wanted it, and if he'd tried to arrange things differently, tried to make her share his life…

His bed.

If he'd tried that, she'd have made it crystal clear she'd meant what she said, that there wouldn't be any sex in this relationship. Why would she want to have sex with him? She'd been carried away that one night but she wasn't ever going to be carried away like that again. Wasn't going to lose control of herself again.

Not ever.

She wasn't going to feel his mouth on hers, his hands on her breasts. She wasn't going to feel the strength of his arms holding her close, or fall asleep with her head cradled on her shoulder, or awaken in the night to the whisper of his breath on her skin, his caress urgent, her response matching that urgency because she wanted him, needed him…

She'd never need anybody.

PLAY 7 Lucky

and get 2 FREE BOOKS and a FREE GIFT

Scratch off the gold area with a coin. Then check below to see the gifts you get!

NO COST! NO OBLIGATION TO BUY! NO PURCHASE NECESSARY!

YES! I have scratched off the gold area. Please send me the **2 FREE BOOKS AND GIFT** for which I qualify. I understand I am under no obligation to purchase any books as explained on the back of this card.

306 HDL DZ42   106 HDL DZ5H

FIRST NAME	LAST NAME

ADDRESS

APT.#	CITY

STATE/PROV.	ZIP/POSTAL CODE

(H-P-04/04)

Worth **2 FREE BOOKS** plus a **FREE GIFT!**

Worth **2 FREE BOOKS!**

Worth **1 FREE BOOK!**

Try Again!

The Harlequin Reader Service® — Here's how it works:

Accepting your 2 free books and gift places you under no obligation to buy anything. You may keep the books and gift and return the shipping statement marked "cancel." If you do not cancel, about a month later we'll send you 6 additional books and bill you just $3.57 each in the U.S., or $4.24 each in Canada, plus 25¢ shipping & handling per book and applicable taxes if any.* That's the complete price and — compared to cover prices of $4.25 each in the U.S. and $4.99 each in Canada — it's quite a bargain! You may cancel at any time, but if you choose to continue, every month we'll send you 6 more books, which you may either purchase at the discount price or return to us and cancel your subscription.

*Terms and prices subject to change without notice. Sales tax applicable in N.Y. Canadian residents will be charged applicable provincial taxes and GST.

She sat up. Cullen took the ice pack away. "Feeling better?"

"Yes. Much. Thank you for your help."

He looked at her, but he didn't move away. Well, she'd move away from him. *Get up,* she told herself. *Marissa, get up...*

Cullen took her hand. "I'll bet you don't have any brothers."

"No. I don't."

"Because if you did, you'd be so used to the sight of gore that it wouldn't mean a thing."

"Really," she said, trying to sound bored but not carrying it off very well. From Vorple blades to brothers and gore, in less than a breath. The man had a gift. What was it the Irish called it? The gift of gab. That's what he had. It was one of the things she'd found charming, the night they'd met. The night he'd made her forget who she was, what she was, made her forget the whole world.

She began to stand up again. Cullen tugged her down beside him again.

"How about sisters? You have any of those?"

"I was an only child," she said stiffly.

"Lucky you."

"Not so lucky," she said, before she could censor herself. "I mean—it must be pleasant, having siblings."

Cullen chuckled. "Siblings, huh? Well, that's certainly better than some of the names I've called 'em. My brothers, especially."

"How many brothers do you have?" Not that it mattered. Nothing about his life mattered, except with regard to the baby inside her, but it was impossible not to ask.

"Two. And three sisters, every last one into what you might call blood sports."

Marissa raised her eyebrows. "Blood sports?"

"Sure. Football, baseball, soccer. It wasn't easy, growing up an O'Connell. My mother was always surprised the local emergency room didn't bolt the doors when they saw us coming.''

A peal of laughter burst from her throat. She hadn't meant it to happen, but she couldn't prevent it. The image of a harried woman followed by a small herd of children with scabby knees approaching a door barred by desperate nurses was just too much.

"There," Cullen said softly, "you see? You do know how to laugh. I'd begun to wonder."

"Cullen, really—"

"I mean, who knows? Girl grew up without a bunch of pain-in-the-butt sisters and brothers around, maybe she'd led such a sheltered life she didn't do much laughing as a kid."

A sheltered life. If he only knew how funny that was. But he wouldn't. She never talked about her childhood. She didn't even like thinking about it. The past was the past. The future was all that mattered. That had been her credo from the time she was old enough to understand that not everyone lived the way she and her mother did.

"Hey."

She looked at Cullen. He'd moved closer to her; his smile was intimate. She felt her heartbeat quicken. When he looked at her like this—when he was close to her like this—

"Why such a serious face?"

Because I think—I think—

"Marissa."

His gaze on her lips felt like a caress.

"Marissa." He cupped her cheek, stroked his thumb lightly over her mouth. "Are you so unhappy here?"

She couldn't meet his eyes. She looked down, saw the hand he'd injured lying, palm up, in his lap. The cut had stopped bleeding, as he'd said, but it looked raw and angry. What she'd told him about her childhood phobia was true enough; she hated the sight of blood and had ever since she'd seen a lifeless man, his shirt stained crimson, lying in the doorway of the apartment house where she lived.

But as Cullen's thumb moved across her lip, she knew that wasn't why she'd been so upset before.

She'd been upset because she'd thought he was hurt. Cullen. Her husband.

"Marissa," he whispered, and when she looked up through her lashes, he bent his head slowly toward hers...

"*¿Esta usted seguro usted tiene todo razón, señora?*"

Cullen turned quickly and saw his housekeeper in the doorway that led to the dining room, hands balled on her plump hips, her round bronzed face knotted with concern. He stared at her in amazement. Concepcion was a woman of few words and she never spoke before she was spoken to. He'd grown accustomed to her reticence; he'd long ago given up trying to get her to say more than yes, no or what shall I leave for your dinner?

Now, in the span of, what, half an hour, she'd said more than she'd said in the three years he'd known her. And she'd interrupted a conversation. Hell, she'd interrupted something far more important, a moment he'd hardly dare imagine might happen.

"What do you want?" He knew his tone was sharp, but he couldn't help it. It didn't help when Marissa drew away from him and rose to her feet.

"*Gracias, Concepcion. Estoy muy bien.*"

"*Este no es el viejo pai, en donde los bebé nacen sin ciudado.*"

"*Sí. Lo sé.*"

"*Entonces usted debe hablar a su marido sobre qué está sucdediendo.*"

"*¡Éste es ninguno de su negocio!*"

"*Usted dice tan, pero estoy libre hablar mi mente.*"

"Are you deaf?" Marissa slipped into angry-sounded English. "I said—"

"Whoa."

Cullen stepped between the women, looked from one to

the other and tried a quick smile to calm things down. It was as useless as ice cubes on a griddle.

"What's going on here?"

Marissa flushed. "It's nothing."

"Give me a break, sweetheart. Concepcion's angry. At you?"

"No. Not at me, exactly." Silence. Then Marissa cleared her throat. "She's from Mexico."

"And?"

"And, I'm half Mexican. My mother was born in Guadalajara."

Cullen decided to ignore the what-do-you-think-of-that belligerence in her tone. He'd tackle that later, after he figured out why a domestic firefight had broken out.

"And?"

"And, since we share a language and, she assumes, a heritage, she thinks she knows what's best for me."

He'd take on that one later, too. God, this was like pulling teeth. *"And?"* Cullen said impatiently.

"She says—"

"The *señora* is pregnant," Concepcion announced.

"And?" Cullen said. "And" seemed to be the only word left in his vocabulary. "Of course she's pregnant. I know that."

"Do you, *señor?*"

"Concepcion!" Marissa's eyes all but shot fire. "That's enough."

"The *señora* needs someone to care for her." The housekeeper glared at Cullen. "You think it is enough you make her your wife, but you do nothing else. You leave her alone all day, you permit her to weep, you don't talk to her—"

"Weep?" Cullen said, staring at Marissa.

Marissa snapped out a sharp command. Concepcion flushed, turned on her heel and marched away.

"I'm sorry," Marissa murmured. "Please don't blame her. She told me she has a daughter my age, back in Mexico. Evidently, she's feeling maternal toward me."

"Weep?" he said again.

Marissa's chin rose. "What does it matter?"

Cullen grabbed Marissa by the shoulders. "Are you crazy? The housekeeper knows that my wife's been crying, but I don't? Of course it matters! Why were you crying?"

"I told you, it doesn't matter."

His mouth thinned. "Because of me. Because of the marriage I demanded."

"No. You were right. Marriage was the right thing. I'll get used to my new life."

Her voice trembled when she said it. Her new life. The life he'd dragged her into. The life he'd done nothing to make welcoming.

God, he was a fool!

Cullen ground out a single, short expletive between his teeth.

"Wait here," he growled, and strode from the room.

"No! Cullen…"

But he marched in the other direction from the kitchen. Concepcion, at least, was safe from his ire.

Marissa sighed. Her shoulders slumped and she sank down on the steps again.

What a mistake she'd made, letting the woman hear her crying that first day. She hadn't intended it to happen; it just had. She'd awakened in this strange place, for a moment so disoriented that she'd thought she was in a bad dream.

Then she'd remembered. Cullen's visit to her apartment. His demands. Her concession to them. The horrid wedding ceremony that had united her to a man who didn't want her but was determined to do the moral thing, the anguish of the flight here with him sitting beside her knotted with tension. This enormous town house with its icily perfect décor.

And Cullen holding her elbow, hurrying her up the stairs to a guest room and abandoning her there because he clearly couldn't wait to be rid of her.

All that night, she lay in a bed that wasn't hers, in a

room that wasn't hers, waiting for the door to open. Waiting for her husband to come to her. To take her in his arms and kiss her and make her see that this marriage could work.

She'd told herself she didn't want him to kiss her. To touch her. It was a lie. When he touched her, oh, when he touched her, everything changed. Her fear, her humiliation at what he made her feel, all disappeared.

Maybe she needed to tell him that, she'd thought, and in those long hours of that endless night, that was what she'd decided to do. She wasn't a coward. She wasn't spineless. Come morning, their first morning as husband and wife, she would tell Cullen she'd thought things over and he was right.

If this marriage had any chance at all, they'd have to behave as if it were real.

She slept a little, awoke early, showered, dried her hair, brushed it until it hung down her back in dark, flowing waves. Then she took a pair of drawstring-waisted silk trousers from her suitcase and topped them with an oversize black cotton T-shirt. At last, she took a deep, deep breath and stepped out into the hall.

Stepped out into her new life…

Alone.

A woman in the kitchen introduced herself curtly as Concepcion, stared at Marissa's belly so hard that Marissa blushed, and handed her a note from Cullen. It was as abrupt as the housekeeper's greeting. He had a meeting he couldn't cancel and he'd see her for dinner.

A meeting he didn't want to cancel and a wife he regretted marrying, was more like it. Even a man who'd done what he called the right thing could come to his senses.

Marissa had crushed the note in her hand.

"The *señor* says you are his wife."

Marissa nodded. "*Sí,*" she'd said automatically, memories of her mother triggered by that familiar accent, "*soy su esposa.*"

Concepcion's face had softened. "You are Mexican?"

Marissa had lifted her eyes to the housckeeper's. "I am nothing," she'd whispered, and the tears had come.

If only she hadn't cried. If only she'd remained strong. She'd never broken down before. Never. Not in the face of her mother's bitterness. Not when the doctor at the clinic had confirmed that she was pregnant. Not when she'd gone to the bursar's office and signed the papers that said she was leaving school, leaving everything she'd ever dreamed of.

Even now, she was weeping. Angrily, she wiped her knuckles over her eyes. Stupid, stupid, stupid. Why had she cried on the first morning of her marriage? Why was she crying now? Why did what Cullen did or didn't do matter?

"Let's go."

Marissa looked up. Cullen was standing over her. He'd shaved away his early-morning stubble.

"Go?" she said blankly. "Go where?"

He reached down, took her hands, lifted her gently to her feet. And he smiled. Oh God, he smiled, and what happened to her foolish, foolish heart when he did was enough to make tears sting her eyes again.

"Out. First to the doctor, then to shop."

"But I'm fine. Really. That fainting spell—"

"A pregnant woman needs to see an obstetrician. I don't know why it took me so long to realize that."

"It's okay. I thought of it. I made some calls… There's a free clinic on—"

"A clinic?"

"Yes. It's not around here, but—"

"I called Ben Silverman. He's one of my partners. He said the obstetrician his wife used is terrific, so I phoned and made an appointment. They were really busy but I said it was important and the receptionist said, well, they'd just had a cancellation and… What?"

"Is this the first you mentioned, uh, the baby and me to anyone?"

Cullen thought about his conversation with Sean, but that didn't count. As far as his brother knew, he'd decided to offer financial support to Marissa and her baby, not marry her.

"Yeah." Color striped his cheeks. "Can you forgive me?" he said softly.

Bewildered, Marissa shook her head. "There's nothing to forgive."

"Of course there is," he said. He sounded angry. With surprise, she realized his anger was for himself. "I coerced you into this marriage and then—then, I chickened out."

"I don't understand."

"Those sisters I mentioned? Bree's into touchy-feely stuff. I think she'd call it, disassociation." Cullen's jaw tightened. "You made it clear you wanted no part of me. And instead of finding ways to make you see I could make you happy, I accepted that and didn't try to change it. I took the out you gave me, and I backed away." He lowered his head to hers, brushed his mouth over hers, did it again and again until he felt her lips soften and cling lightly to his. "Marissa. This is as new to me as it is to you. I'm every bit as scared but, damn it, we'll find a way to make it work."

"I don't—"

"I know. I don't know, either. The only thing I'm sure of is that we have to give it a try."

She sighed. He was right. "For the baby," she said quietly.

"For him. And for us. The thought of you weeping, of you feeling so alone, breaks my heart." Cullen tunneled his fingers into her hair, tilted her face up to his. "As for the practicalities of this new life... How could I have been such a fool? It's not enough to give you a roof over your head. You need a doctor. Clothing. Whatever it is makes women look in the mirror and smile."

"No. I have—"

"Don't argue with me," he said firmly. "We're going to the doctor. Then we're going shopping. You got that?"

"The doctor, yes. But not the rest. I don't need anything."

Cullen smiled. He hated himself for his stupidity. His insensitivity. His cowardice. But he loved hearing the way Marissa was talking. The way she was lifting that chin and looking right at him.

Yes. Oh yes. Tucked away inside, his bright, beautiful, stubborn Marissa had only been waiting to emerge.

She was still talking, telling him why she wouldn't spend his money. He decided not to waste energy arguing. It was easier and far, far more satisfying to silence this woman the only way that seemed to work.

He kissed her, felt her tremble as he did.

Then Cullen put his arm around his wife's shoulders and led her into the world.

CHAPTER EIGHT

IF SOMEBODY had asked Cullen to name ten of his favorite pastimes, sitting in the crowded waiting room of a doctor's office wouldn't have made the list.

Thankfully, he hadn't spent much time in places like that. Immunization shots before a post-Princeton, pre-Berkeley, around-the-world backpacking trip. A banged-up knee, courtesy of a losing argument with a recalcitrant halyard on his boat. A dislocated shoulder, a badge of honor he'd acquired during an our-office-against-yours, no-holds-barred racquetball tournament.

What he remembered from those infrequent stops in doctors' waiting rooms were outdated magazines, elevator music, and somebody always sitting right beside him, coughing like a character in the final act of a bad opera.

This visit wasn't like that.

Ben had recommended an obstetrician in the Back Bay area. Cullen lucked out and got a parking spot on the first try.

"That's a small miracle," he said, hoping to lighten the atmosphere, but it didn't work. Marissa didn't respond. She opened her door and got out before he could open it for her.

The doctor's office was in a redbrick version of Boston's most estimable dowagers: dignified, well-maintained, attractive enough to remind you that it must have been a beauty among beauties in its youth. Boxes of flowers hung at the windowsills; the black wooden door sported a brass door-knocker for show and a discreet buzzer for actual use.

"Looks pretty good," Cullen said, still trying for the right tone.

Marissa still didn't say anything. He wasn't surprised. She hadn't spoken a word all the way here. He was pretty sure he understood the reason. Understood it? Hell, he felt it, same as she did.

The wedding ceremony, though legal, had been pure Las Vegas. As such, it had seemed unreal.

This wasn't. There was nothing unreal about Cullen O'Connell and wife, parents-to-be, visiting an obstetrician together.

For a heartbeat, Cullen thought about turning tail and running.

What stopped him wasn't anything as grand as Doing What Was Right. It was simply the look on Marissa's face. She was as terrified as he was. Maybe more. She was the one carrying a child neither of them had planned, the one who'd been torn from her world...

Cullen cleared his throat. "Let's do it," he said.

He took her hand, half expecting her to pull away. To his amazement, she threaded her fingers through his. He looked down. The top of her head came just to his shoulder. She was so small. So helpless...

So beautiful and determined, even now, her chin up, her eyes straight ahead.

"Marissa."

She looked at him. From somewhere deep inside, Cullen dredged up a smile.

"It's going to be fine," he said.

She nodded. Still no words, but a nod was an improvement over silence.

Cullen took a breath, pressed the buzzer, opened the door... And stepped onto an alien planet.

Women. The waiting room was crammed with them. They sat side by side by side on a pair of black leather sofas, perched on the ladder-backed chairs ranged along two walls; one leaned against the receptionist's desk.

Nothing but women, Cullen thought dazedly, and they all had one thing in common.

Each sported a huge belly.

Cullen froze. He was just getting used to having a pregnant wife. This seemed dangerously close to more than a man could handle.

Marissa spoke her first words in an hour. "You can wait outside, if you like," she murmured, as if she'd read his mind.

Cullen swallowed hard. "No," he said briskly, "why would I want to do that?"

Why, indeed?

DR. STERN wasn't.

Stern, that was.

That was Cullen's first thought. Stern had a ruddy face, a booming voice and a big smile. He was middle-aged, a big guy who looked like he'd played football in his college days. When it was time for Marissa's appointment, he came to the waiting room door himself.

"Mrs. O'Connell?"

For a second, neither Cullen nor Marissa moved. Then Marissa jerked to her feet. *Mrs. O'Connell?* Cullen thought in amazement. Nobody had called her that yet, not in his presence.

"I'm Dr. Stern. Come in, please. You, too, Mr. O'Connell."

Me, too?

"We don't bite, Mr. O'Connell," Stern assured him.

The other women in the waiting room smiled appreciatively. Cullen felt his face redden.

"It's my wife who has the appointment," he said, wincing at the stupidity of the words as Stern let the door swing shut behind them.

It turned out Stern was more than pleasant. He was kind, as well.

"Of course," he said gently. "But whenever possible, I like to meet the husband. After all, this is your baby, too."

My baby, too, Cullen thought. *My baby, too...*

"Yes," he said, and cleared his throat. "Yes, it is."

The doctor led them into a small office paneled in light wood. Framed diplomas and certificates hung on one wall; the other was crammed with snapshots of newborns.

"My alumni," Stern said cheerfully, waving to the pictures.

Cullen stared at all those small, screwed-up faces. The knot in his gut took another turn. It was probably a Gordian knot by now. This was the real thing. Babies-in-the-flesh, not in the belly.

Could he handle this? Marriage, and now fatherhood?

"Cute little kids, huh?"

Cullen stared at the doctor's smiling face. "Yeah," he said hoarsely. "Cute."

"So." Stern motioned them to chairs, settled in behind his desk, folded his hands on his stomach and smiled at Marissa. "Mrs. O'Connell. Or may I call you Marissa? Good. Tell me about yourself, Marissa. I understand you've only recently moved east. I assume you've been under someone else's care?"

The doctor asked questions. Marissa's medical history, which was uneventful. Questions about her family history. Her mother. Her father, which elicited a tense, "I don't know anything about my father."

It caught Cullen by surprise, though he didn't show it. But it explained a lot. A woman who'd never known her old man might very well expect the same treatment from the guy who'd made her pregnant.

What kind of SOB would turn his back on a woman? On a helpless baby? He wanted to pull his wife from her chair, hold her in his arms...

"...since you didn't bring any records with you, we'll put in a request to your prior physician and ask him to forward the data to my office. With your permission, of course.''

Marissa nodded. ''It might take a while,'' she said softly. ''I mean, the doctors I saw before… It was a public clinic, and they were always very crowded.''

Stern's eyebrows lifted. ''Oh?''

Cullen felt a muscle jump in his jaw. There was a world of meaning in that ''oh.''

''Well, I've known clinics that do a fine job. It's just, well, you're right. It might take a while to get data from them.'' Stern looked from Marissa to Cullen. ''I'm assuming they did an ultrasound?''

''Yes.''

''And the baby was fine?''

''Yes. An ultrasound…and an amniocentesis.''

''Why? Did they see a problem in the ultrasound?''

Marissa could hear the sudden change in Dr. Stern's tone, the sharpening of those twinkling eyes behind the wire-rimmed glasses. She knew what she should say. *They did it because my husband wanted a paternity test…* But the words were so ugly that she couldn't get them past her lips.

Suddenly, Cullen reached for her hand, his fingers squeezing hers in reassurance.

''It was just procedural,'' he said smoothly. ''There were no problems, Doctor.''

Stern nodded. Then he leaned across his desk.

''I'm sure you're right. But in view of the fact that it's apparently going to take a while to get those records…would either of you object to my doing another ultrasound? We can do it right now. And, as you undoubtedly already know, it's perfectly harmless to the baby and mother.''

Cullen looked at his wife. ''Marissa?'' he said quietly.

She turned to him. ''It's expensive,'' she whispered, her face heating. ''The technician at the clinic said—''

''Do it,'' Cullen told Stern.

"Excellent." Stern rose to his feet. "Tell you what, Mr. O'Connell. I'll have a look at your wife. And when we're ready for the ultrasound, I'll have my nurse come and collect you."

"Me?" Cullen said stupidly.

"Certainly." The doctor grinned. "I'm sure you'll want a second look at that baby of yours."

"Oh, but—" *But what? I never had a first look? I didn't even know the baby existed until a few weeks ago?* "Of course," Cullen said smoothly. "That'll be—it'll be great."

TIME crawled by.

The nurse popped in with a couple of magazines.

"Thought these might keep you busy," she said cheerfully, and shut the door before Cullen could answer.

Busy? Reading *Beautiful Babies* and the *Parenting News*? He opened one magazine, saw all those pictures of all those tiny infants looking helpless and totally dependent.

Sweet Jesus.

Sweat broke out on his forehead. He closed the magazine, closed his eyes, too.

What in hell was he doing here? How come he hadn't thought ahead? Why hadn't he figured agreeing to be a father to this child meant sitting in a doctor's office surrounded by pictures of rug rats?

Surrounded by pictures, and waiting to see pictures of his own. Fuzzy images of an unidentifiable something.

Hey, he'd seen those programs on the Discovery channel. A woman lying on a table. A tech standing beside her. A photo on a TV screen, and an oily voice explaining the unexplainable.

This is a baby in its mother's uterus. Do you see its head? Its heart? Its hands?

No, no, and no. Leaning forward, eyes focused on the TV set, all any sensible viewer could see was a featureless blob…

"Mr. O'Connell?" The cheerful nurse was back.

"Yeah." Cullen sprang to his feet. The magazine slipped, unnoticed, to the floor. "Look, I know you must be very busy. I mean, fitting my wife in like this— So, I'll just go into the waiting room and—"

"Doctor's ready for you, sir."

Cullen nodded. No way out, he thought, and walked down a hall that was surely a mile long, stepped into a small room, saw Marissa lying on a table, just like he'd expected, saw the smooth curve of her belly, saw a TV screen...

And saw his son, peacefully adrift within his wife's sheltering womb. Saw his boy's ten tiny fingers and ten tiny toes. Saw his big, dark eyes and damned well felt them grab his heart with a feeling so intense he felt tears burn his eyes.

Cullen sank into the chair beside his wife and reached for her hand.

He wanted to say something clever. Something meaningful, that they'd both remember forever.

But Marissa squeezed his hand, gave him a wobbly smile, and all he could do was lean down and kiss her mouth.

"Our son," he said, his voice as scratchy as if his throat were coated with dust.

And for the very first time since his sixth birthday, when his mother had said, yes, he could keep the puppy he'd found abandoned in a weedy lot near the miserable place they'd been living, Cullen O'Connell unashamedly wept.

CULLEN left the doctor's office carrying a wicker basket laden with little sample boxes and bottles of oils, soaps, lotions and creams. Brochures were stuffed in his pockets on every subject from childbirth to the hospital where the baby would be born. A schedule for Lamaze classes was tucked in his appointment book.

Marissa watched him balance the basket in the crook of

one arm as he popped the Porsche's trunk. The basket was small to start with but it looked positively Lilliputian, cradled against her husband's hard, masculine body.

Her husband.

The word sent a little shiver of pleasure along her spine. Strange, but until today she hadn't really let herself think of him that way. He'd been Cullen, or the man she lived with, or the man she'd married.

Now, in the blink of an eye, she found herself thinking of him by another name.

Her husband.

"Okay," he said, as he shut the trunk lid. "All safely stowed away." He looked at her and grinned. "It's gonna take us hours to go through it."

She smiled. "Uh-huh."

"We'll probably need an interpreter, too."

"You think?"

"I know." He helped her into the car, then went around to the driver's side and got behind the wheel. "For instance, there's a coupon right on the top for something called a Onesie." He looked at her as he turned the ignition key and flashed a quick smile. "You have any idea what in heck a Onesie is?"

"A little undershirt and diaper thingy," Marissa said, laughing when Cullen arched his eyebrows. "Honest, that's what it is. I looked at baby clothes before— I looked at them in Berkeley."

"Ah. Well, I suspect I'm going to be on new territory here." Cullen checked his mirror and pulled away from the curb. "What I know about babies you could cram into a nutshell and still have space left for a hanging judge's heart."

"No nieces or nephews in your family?"

"Not yet. Getting close, though. Keir—my older brother—Keir and his wife are expecting any day now."

"Oh."

Marissa fell silent. Cullen looked at her. He cleared his

throat. "You'll have to meet them soon. My family, I mean."

"Have you—have you told them about us?"

"No. Not yet. I keep waiting for the right time."

"I understand." Marissa shot him a tight smile. "It's not easy to tell the people who love you that you had to marry a woman because—"

Cullen yanked the wheel hard to the right and stopped at the curb.

"I didn't have to marry you," he said gruffly. "I chose to, the same as you chose to marry me."

"Because it was the right thing," she said softly, and looked at him.

Their eyes met, hers searching his for an answer to a question she hadn't asked. And yet, somehow, he thought he might know the answer as well as the question.

The moment slipped by. Then Cullen started the car again and merged into traffic.

"Yes," he said, even more gruffly. "It was."

Marissa nodded and folded her hands together in her lap. "So," she said, after another few seconds of silence, "what did you think?"

"About the ultrasound?" Cullen puffed out a breath. "It's the most incredible thing I've ever seen. He was sucking his thumb. Did you see that?"

She smiled. "The tech said maybe that's what he was doing."

"He was," Cullen said positively. "And then he turned his head. Looked straight at me." He grinned. "Absolutely incredible. I just never expected it to be like that. So clear. So—so—"

"Incredible," Marissa said, and they smiled at each other until his smile faded and died.

"Can you forgive me?"

"For what?"

"For not being there for you from the beginning."

"That was my doing, not yours."

"No more talking about that. We made mistakes, but we're past them." He paused. "Aren't we?"

Marissa nodded. He was right. The time for reliving the past was over. And yes, today had been incredible...

Especially the way her husband had looked at her when he came into the ultrasound screening room.

She loved having him look at her that way, as if what had happened was what he'd wanted all along. As if they'd met and fallen in love the way people did in storybooks, married because they couldn't live without each other, planned this new life because it was the best possible celebration of their love.

Never mind. He was right. They could make this marriage work. And oh, she wanted it to work. Wanted it, wanted it...

"You know what I'm thinking?" Cullen said.

Marissa looked at him. "What?"

"We have to celebrate. Go out to lunch. Someplace special. But we'll have to pass on champagne. The doctor said no alcohol, no caffeine, no—"

"I haven't had any of those things since I learned I was pregnant."

"Yeah." Cullen's smile tilted. "But this is all new to me."

It was new to her, too, sharing the pregnancy with someone. For months, she'd kept it a secret, ashamed to let her professors know, afraid to let her boss know. Now, all at once, she was sharing it with Cullen.

With her husband.

Marissa's heart skittered into her throat. She felt close to tears. Silly, of course. Theirs was a practical arrangement, nothing more. Why would she want to weep? Hormones, that was the reason, all that pregnancy-related estrogen pumping through her body like a river in full flood.

"What do you feel like having? Lobster? A salad? I know this little place down near the harbor—"

Hormones or not, she was living a dream. This man

who'd filled her thoughts for so long was hers. They were really married. Crazy as it seemed, she hadn't actually let it hit her until today.

"Marissa? Sweetheart, you're not listening to me. Aren't you hungry?" He turned a worried face toward her. "You're not feeling sick, are you?"

"No, no. I'm fine."

"In that case, we'll head for the harbor. I'm starved. And you need to eat. You heard what the doctor said."

"He said I'm fine."

"He said you could stand to gain some weight."

"He only said that after *you* said you thought I was too thin."

"Look, I know you don't like being told what to do, but—"

No. She didn't. At least, she never had before. But this was different. Cullen wasn't telling her what to do so much as he was telling her that she mattered to him.

She liked that. She loved it. She might not take his advice but there was something special in knowing a man cared enough about you to be concerned for your welfare...

Except, Cullen was concerned about the baby. About his son, not about her. She wanted only the best for their child, too, but—but she wanted her husband to think about her as a woman, not only as the mother of his baby.

Marissa's throat constricted.

What was happening to her? For two weeks she'd avoided any contact with Cullen. She'd been filled with anger over the turn her life had taken, even though part of her knew that accepting the marriage he'd forced on her was the only logical choice.

Now, just because Cullen had held her hand during the ultrasound exam, because he'd had tears in his eyes watching their child move inside her, she was on the verge of becoming a woman who was soft and stupid when it came to men. A woman she'd sworn she'd never be.

No. That wouldn't happen.

Marissa sat up straight. "You're right," she said coolly. "I don't like being told what to do."

Cullen reached for her hand. She tried to jerk it back, but his fingers closed around hers.

"Okay. How's this sound? You're not too thin. You just need a couple of pounds to make you even more beautiful."

"Give it up, Cullen," Marissa snapped. "I don't need to eat more than I already do, and I'm far from beautiful. If anything, I look like a beached whale."

Cullen chuckled. What was wrong with the man? Didn't he know when he was being dismissed?

Ahead, a traffic light went from green to red. He pulled to a stop, brought her hand to his mouth and pressed a kiss to it.

"A beautiful whale."

Oh, the feel of his mouth against her skin. Did he know what his caress did to her? That she could feel herself melting? That it made her want to throw herself into his arms?

She wouldn't. She couldn't. It was dangerous to feel this way. She'd always known that and yet, look what she'd done that fateful night? Lost control, turned into her mother's daughter, and lost everything she'd planned.

It wasn't that she didn't love her baby. She did, with all her heart. She was even willing to admit that Cullen was a decent man, but this marriage had nothing to do with feelings. It had to do with his sense of honor, his sense of responsibility...and her vulnerability.

Their relationship would be reviewed every two years. And whenever her husband lost his enthusiasm for matrimony or for her, she'd be gone like yesterday's garbage. Only a fool would forget that little detail, and she was never going to be a fool with this man again.

Marissa tugged her hand from Cullen's and smoothed down her skirt. "It must be wonderful," she said without looking at him, "being able to rely on all that blarney."

"No blarney, sweetheart, just the truth. What could be lovelier than the sight of my wife, ripe with our child?"

His wife. Their child. It sounded so wonderful. So perfect. If only—if only—

"I know just the place for lunch," he said softly.

"I'm not hungry."

"Well, I am." He shot her a smile. "Come on. Loosen up. I told you, I want to take you somewhere special to celebrate."

"And I want to go back to the town house."

Cullen looked over at his wife's unyielding profile. That chin was up, cocked at an angle he knew meant trouble. What in hell had happened? It had to be hormones. He recalled Keir rolling his eyes and saying Cassie was driving him crazy, sugar-sweet one minute, acerbic and unreasonable the next.

Okay. He wouldn't leap to the bait. If Marissa wanted a quarrel, she wouldn't get one from him.

"Tell you what," he said, as the light went green. "We'll drive out of town. I know this little place on the coast—"

"I'll tell *you* what," Marissa replied. "We'll drive back to your town house."

Cullen's mouth narrowed. Take it easy, he told himself. Just take it nice and easy...

To hell with nice and easy.

"*The* town house," he said coldly. "*My* town house. Has it occurred to you that it's *our* town house? Our home?"

"No. It hasn't. And it isn't. Does that answer your question?"

Cullen's hands tightened on the wheel. Was it impossible for Marissa to spend more than a few minutes in his company without regretting it?

"You don't see anything to celebrate today?"

"My son is healthy. That's celebration enough for me."

"*Our* son," Cullen said grimly. "Why do you keep forgetting that?"

"How can I forget? You won't let me."

"That's it," he snarled. "I've had enough." And in a

decision made in a heartbeat, he swung onto a highway entrance ramp that would take them out of the city, put his foot down on the gas pedal and started the eighty mile drive to Hyannis, and the plane that would take them to his house on Nantucket Island.

CHAPTER NINE

ALMOST an hour later, the sign flashed by so quickly Marissa almost missed it.

Cape Cod.

Was that where they were going? And if so, why?

She had no idea.

Cullen hadn't said a word since leaving Boston. She'd wasted five minutes insisting he tell her what in hell he thought he was doing before she'd realized she was not only wasting her breath, she was playing into his hands. Her demand for answers was just what he wanted. So she'd clamped her lips together and sat back in stony silence.

He'd stopped only once, at a gas station outside the city. He'd filled the tank, made a show of taking the keys from the ignition and marched into the station's convenience store.

A damn good thing he'd taken the keys, she'd thought coldly, because his suspicion was right. She'd have driven off and left him.

He returned carrying two containers of coffee and two wrapped sandwiches.

"Decaf," he'd said, putting one container and one sandwich on the console beside her.

So, yes. Correction. He *had* spoken during the past hour, but just that one word, as if to remind her of what she already knew, that she was pregnant and carrying his child and because of that, she was in his control.

Of course, she'd ignored all of it. Him, the coffee and the sandwich. He'd pretty much done the same thing, making a face and putting aside his sandwich after just one bite...

Even that one bite was more than she'd had.

Her stomach was growling, though it seemed ridiculous to feel something as commonplace as hunger when you were being carried off to God only knew where by a man who thought a couple of smiles and a handful of "sweethearts" would turn you to clay in his hands.

Another sign zipped by. *Hyannis.* The name seemed vaguely familiar. Didn't some president have a home in Hyannis a long time ago? Ford. Johnson. Kennedy. That was it. Kennedy.

Not that she cared.

She wasn't much in the mood for visiting historical sights, Marissa thought coldly, and sat even straighter in her seat.

Damn it, why didn't he say anything? Another minute and she'd ask, even though she hated giving him the satisfaction.

There went sign number three. *Barnstable Airport.*

Airport?

Okay. That did it. Being taken on a car ride to nowhere was bad enough, but if Cullen thought she was getting on a plane and heading into the blue without knowing their destination, he was crazy.

"All right," she said, swinging toward him. "That's it. I've never been a fan of mystery tours, Cullen. What are we doing here?"

"Think hard enough," he said, pulling into a parking space, "and I'll bet you'll figure it out."

"Do you expect me to get on a plane with you?"

"You see?" His voice was cool as he opened his door, came around the car and opened hers. "I knew you'd come up with the answer."

He held out his hand. Marissa didn't move.

"If you think I'm getting on a jet without knowing where—"

"It's not a jet, it's a prop job. And I told you where we're going. Out to lunch."

"We already had lunch."

"We did not." Cullen glanced at his watch. "Get out of the car, please, Marissa. We're wasting time."

"No."

"You're behaving like a child."

"I'm behaving like an adult in charge of her own life. I'm not getting out of this car."

"One," Cullen said calmly.

"This is ridiculous! You have no right—"

"Two."

"Do you really think you can force me into—"

"Three," he said, reaching across her to the seat belt lock. Marissa slapped at his hands but he ignored her, undid the belt and pulled it back. "Let's go."

"I told you and told you, I am not—"

Her words ended in a shriek as Cullen lifted her into his arms and pushed the door shut with his hip.

"Damn you, O'Connell!"

"Probably," he said calmly. "It's up to you, lady. Do you walk, or do I carry you?" He jerked his head to the side. "We seem to specialize in having audiences. What this one sees or not is your choice."

Marissa glared at him, then shifted her gaze to a small building with *Michael's Air Taxi* painted on its side. A couple of men were standing near the door, watching them with interest.

Fine, she thought. Let them watch. Let them see that Cullen O'Connell was a bullying idiot.

"Well? Are you going to behave?"

Her reply was a string of Spanish words, delivered too rapidly for him to understand, and accompanied by fists pounding against his shoulder.

Cullen grunted. "Whatever," he said, and marched toward the building.

She slammed another fist into his shoulder and spat out

something about him having the intelligence of a dim-witted gorilla.

Creative, he thought grimly, and probably true. This had been a class-A stupid idea.

The more miles the Porsche ate up during the drive from Boston to the Cape, the clearer that truth had become. He'd never brought anyone here, to this one place in the world that mattered to him. He'd grown up in falling-down cottages beside weed-infested lakes, in apartments that were almost duplicates of the one where he'd found Marissa. After his old man finally hit it big, he'd lived in the anonymity of the huge owner's suite at the Desert Song Hotel.

His town house in Boston was almost as big, surely as handsome, and absolutely as anonymous.

The place they'd fly to, if Marissa ever shut up, was the only place he'd ever thought of as home.

Then, why was he bringing her there? She hated his town house, hated Boston, hated him.

Cullen strode the last few yards toward the air taxi office. Marissa had fallen dangerously silent, but that didn't keep the two guys standing outside the building from grinning like hyenas.

"Afternoon," one of them said pleasantly.

The other gave Cullen a mock salute and opened the door.

Cullen grunted his thanks and stepped inside. Mike, who owned the place and had surely observed every bit of the little performance through the window, raised his eyebrows.

"Nice to see you again, Mr. O'Connell," he said conversationally. "Flying to the island today, are you?"

Cullen eased Marissa to her feet but kept one arm tightly wrapped around her waist. Her silence was, he suspected, ominous. She wasn't a woman to give up so easily. If trying to beat his shoulders to pulp and calling down what he suspected was the wrath of the Aztec gods of her ancestors on his head hadn't accomplished what she wanted, he figured her best effort was yet to come.

"Yeah," he growled, "nice to see you, too. You have two seats available on the next flight?"

Mike scratched his ear. "Reckon so."

"Fine. We'll take them."

"He means, he'll take one of the seats," Marissa said.

Here we go, Cullen thought, looking at his wife. Oh yes, something was coming. She lifted her chin any higher, she wouldn't be able to see over it.

"Two," he said quietly.

"One," Marissa repeated. "Just one seat to wherever it is you're going, Mike."

"Nantucket, unless Mr. O'Connell here's changed his usual flight destination."

"Frankly," Marissa said pleasantly, "I don't care if Mr. O'Connell is flying to Nantucket, whatever that is—"

"It's an island," the air taxi owner said helpfully. "'Bout 30 miles south of here."

"I don't care if he flies to Nantucket or Naples. All I know is that I'm not going with him."

Cullen stretched his lips into a smile.

"Meet my wife."

"I am not his wife. I mean, I am, but I'm not…" Marissa drew a labored breath. "Do you fly to Boston?"

"Well," Mike said with caution, "we don't, no. But over in the terminal—"

"Excuse us a minute, would you, Mike?" Cullen clamped a hand around Marissa's wrist and drew her into a corner. "We're not going back to Boston," he said coldly. "We're going to Nantucket."

"You can go where you like. I'm going to Boston."

"Really," Cullen said, turning the word into a sarcastic statement. "And how are you going to do that? You don't have a credit card, and don't bother lying because I checked. You canceled your credit cards when you quit school, which is why I opened new accounts for you, but you ignored the cards I left for you the other morning."

"I'll pay cash. Remember? That dirty green stuff people like you don't like to touch."

"I like that dirty green stuff just fine," Cullen said coldly, "but you haven't got enough to buy lunch, much less an airplane ticket."

"You don't know that."

Her chin was still angled in the air but there was a quaver of uncertainty in her voice. It made him feel like the son of a bitch he undoubtedly was, but it was too late to stop now.

"I do," he said, and told her the fare. Actually, he made up a number, but so what? His wife wasn't going back to Boston. She wasn't going anyplace. Not yet. He didn't have any idea why he'd dragged her here but she was here, and, damn it all, she wasn't going to leave until he'd figured out the reason. "See what I mean? Like it or not, you're stuck with me and my island."

STUCK? Trapped, was more like it, but what choice did she have?

None, Marissa thought bitterly, as the black SUV that had been waiting at the Nantucket airstrip bounced along a narrow road.

At least it turned out Cullen had been talking figuratively when he referred to "his island." This wasn't a private island, thank God. There were other homes, a town, roads. She'd feared they were going to be put down on a rock in the middle of the Atlantic, but obviously Nantucket was a civilized place.

A place the man she'd married knew well.

He was driving the SUV, shifting gears, taking lefts and rights in a way that told her he'd spent a lot of time in this place.

"Get in," he'd said brusquely, and when she hadn't moved quickly enough to satisfy his lordship, he'd lifted her up again, put her in her seat and started to buckle her in. She'd balked at that, slapping his hands away as she had when he'd reached across her to open her seat belt at the parking lot near the air taxi office.

Opening that belt, his hand had brushed over her breasts. She wasn't going to let that happen again.

She knew the act hadn't been deliberate. She knew, too, that her breasts were far more sensitive than usual, thanks to her pregnancy. Still, that swift whisper of Cullen's fingers over her nipples had made the muscles low in her belly clench like a fist.

Hormones. A simple chemical reaction. He was the closest thing she'd ever known to a tyrant but even if her head knew that, her body didn't. Cullen was a good-looking man. All right. He was a gorgeous hunk, and she reacted to him even though she despised him.

All it proved was that she was no better than other women who were at the mercy of their libidos. She was equally vulnerable, equally stupid, but she was ahead of the game for knowing it.

Not that she had anything to worry about.

Marissa shot Cullen another quick look.

No. She had nothing to fear on that account. She had no idea why he'd brought her to this place but it certainly had nothing to do with seduction.

No sex. That had been her stipulation to his contract terms. And he hadn't touched her. Two weeks of marriage, and nothing. They slept in separate beds in separate rooms. She was happy for that. Of course she was. She wouldn't have let him touch her. If he'd come to her in the dark of night, when she lay in the silence thinking about him, if he'd come to her then, said her name, sat on the bed next to her and lifted her into his arms, she'd have—she'd have stopped him.

Absolutely, she'd have stopped him.

Marissa swallowed past the sudden dryness in her throat. She remembered what he'd done, all those months ago. His hands on her. His mouth on her. Why would she want any of that? She was a decent woman. Just because she'd slipped once…

Slipped big time, she thought, and lightly pressed a hand to her belly.

No, she didn't want Cullen. What she wanted was the baby sleeping in her womb. Cullen wanted him, too. That was the only reason he'd married her. She had to remember that. Otherwise…

Otherwise, her husband could break her heart because—because—

Her breath caught. Don't go there, she told herself frantically. Not now, not ever.

The SUV jerked to a stop. "There's the house," Cullen said.

Marissa blinked and stared blindly at his face, his features lit by the gold of the late-afternoon sun. A smile curved his mouth, his beautiful mouth. She recalled the feel of it on her skin, and suddenly she knew that she should have returned to Boston even if she'd had to walk.

"Where?" she said, grateful now for the interruption, willing to talk, to do anything but let her mind lead her to a place she would not, could not go. "I don't see—"

And then she did.

It was an old, gray-shingled house, weathered by the wind, and stood on a rise of sun-bleached grasses. Before it, pale golden sand stretched toward a deep blue sea.

"Oh," she said, without thinking, "oh, Cullen, it's beautiful."

Cullen looked at her. She was leaning forward, face shining, eyes fixed on the cottage he'd restored with his own hands, and he let out a breath he hadn't known he was holding.

"Yeah," he said gruffly. "I think so, too."

He turned into the long driveway, slowed the car to a crawl and took this last bit of the trip slowly, as he always did. It was his way of shedding the attorney's skin he wore in Boston.

Now, he drove slowly for an even more important reason.

He wanted to give Marissa time to see his home. Her home. To absorb the silence, broken only by the sighing of the wind. To feel the seclusion of his untouched five acres of moors and beyond, the endless sea.

His jaw tightened.

And wasn't that pathetic? She'd said the house was beautiful, but so what? He'd seen photos of the moon that were beautiful. That didn't mean he wanted to spend a weekend there.

He had no neighbors. No TV. No phone, except for his cell, and his secretary knew she'd damn well better call him only in the event of an emergency.

Once he reached this place, he was isolated. He liked it that way. Marissa wouldn't. Hell, she'd come prepared to hate it, the same way she obviously still hated him. This morning's respite hadn't meant a thing.

Stupid. Stupid to have dragged her here.

Cullen gritted his teeth and gave the SUV more juice. Okay. He'd pause at the house just long enough for her to have time to rest. The doctor had given her a clean bill of health but driving a pregnant woman from one end of Massachusetts to the other probably wasn't the smartest thing he'd ever done. After that, he'd apologize for his actions, turn the SUV around, drive straight to the airport—

"A rabbit," Marissa said, in tones of such delight that Cullen looked at her.

She was smiling. Smiling!

He felt an answering smile curve his lips.

"You like rabbits?"

Brilliant, O'Connell. A totally brilliant conversational gambit...but his wife seemed to think it was.

"Oh, yes. There was a little park, when I was growing up..."

"Yeah?"

"Nothing. I just, I mean, I used to see rabbits there sometimes."

Cullen nodded. "Well, there are lots of rabbits on these moors."

"Moors?" She looked at him, still smiling. "You mean, like in *Wuthering Heights*?"

He had no idea what was in *Wuthering Heights,* but he wasn't about to disagree.

"Right. That's what they call the meadows on this island. Moors." He cleared his throat. "We have deer, too." Her smile broadened. "And seals and sea turtles sometimes turn up on the beach," he said, feeling like a daddy putting his kid's gifts under the tree on Christmas eve.

"I've never— I mean, in Berkeley—"

"Uh-huh. Not much wildlife in Boston, either, or in Vegas."

"Vegas?"

"Las Vegas. Where I grew up…"

Damn. He was babbling. But that look on his wife's face. That softness in her voice. She'd smiled like this, sounded like this, only two times since they'd met. This morning, while they'd watched the ultrasound pictures of their son…and a lifetime ago, that night they'd made love.

He pulled into the garage that was attached to the house, turned off the engine and waited.

Something was happening. He could feel it. Something inside him. He was close, so close to knowing why he'd insisted on bringing Marissa here, what he wanted from this place, from her…

"Marissa?"

"Yes?"

"Marissa, look at me."

A second passed. Then she did as he'd asked but in that intervening bit of time, everything had changed. The set of her mouth, the look in her eyes… She was looking at him as if he were a stranger next to her on a train.

"Yes?"

Cullen felt his smile fade. "Nothing," he said curtly, and the mystery of why he'd come here with Marissa closed around him again like fog rolling in from the sea.

HE'D phoned the couple who watched the place for him from the gas station, asked them to lay in some supplies, so there was steak and salad for supper, eggs and bacon for breakfast.

But he hadn't thought beyond that.

He kept clothes here—jeans, shirts, hiking boots, sneakers—but there wasn't a thing a woman could wear.

He'd never brought a woman here.

His wife was the first. He thought about telling her that as she stood in the center of the living room, her arms wrapped around herself, but decided against it. Why tell her something that wouldn't matter a damn to her? He didn't really know why it should matter to him.

Instead, he lit a match to the kindling and logs on the hearth of the big stone fireplace that dominated the room.

"Bedrooms are upstairs," he said briskly, as he rose to his feet and turned to her. "There's a bathroom up there, too, and a powder room just off the kitchen, if you want to freshen up."

"Which bedroom?"

"Sorry?"

"Which bedroom is mine?"

She asked the question in the tone you'd use with a bellman who'd shown you to a suite of rooms in a hotel.

"Either one," he said tightly.

"Perhaps I should have phrased it more clearly. Which room is yours?"

"The one that overlooks the beach."

"Fine." Her smile was quick and polite. "I'll take the other one."

He nodded. "Yeah," he said, and before he let himself say anything else, he swung back to the fireplace, put one foot on the stepped-up hearth, and glared into the flames.

An hour later, he knocked on her door.

"I have some stuff that might fit you. Jeans of mine, a couple of shirts."

He waited for an answer. There was none. Mouth thinning, he draped the clothing over the balcony railing outside the door.

"Dinner in fifteen minutes," he said.

That, at least, drew a response.

"I'm not hungry."

"You haven't eaten since breakfast."

"I said—"

"I heard what you said. You're eating for two now. Either you come down in fifteen minutes or I'll come up and get you."

Marissa glared at the closed door. It wasn't bad enough Cullen had her trapped in Boston. Now he had her trapped here, in a house in the middle of nowhere, a house not half the size of his town house, meaning they'd probably trip over each other for however long he insisted on keeping her here.

And wasn't it a pity? Because this house was a wonderful place.

Wonderful, she thought, and turned blindly to the window and the sea of beach grass. How many women had Cullen brought here? Made love to, before the fireplace or in the enormous bed in the master bedroom she'd looked into as she came up the stairs? There was a skylight over the bed. You could probably lie in his arms at night and count the stars.

Count the times he took you up to those stars, held you there, trembling on the brink of release.

Marissa sank down on the edge of the bed.

Why had he brought her here? She couldn't think of any reason that made sense. Surely not to count the stars, or lie in his arms, or laugh and hold hands and walk the empty beaches.

Did he think he could seduce her? Get her into his bed,

as he'd at first promised, when he'd told her he wanted her to marry him?

She turned and looked at herself in the mirror. No, she thought, no, there wasn't anything to worry about when it came to that. What man would want a woman who looked like this? If a man loved his woman, that would be different. He'd see the changes in her body as beautiful, but this marriage wasn't about love, it was about expediency and doing what was right and—

"Time's up." Cullen banged his fist against the door.

Not yet, Marissa thought. But sooner or later, it would be. Two years. And for all she knew, he wouldn't even wait that long to get rid of her.

Tears blurred her vision. She wiped them away, got to her feet, took a deep breath, and went to the door.

THEY ate on a small table set before the fireplace. The meal, Marissa thought, was probably delicious.

Cullen had grilled steaks on the hearth; he'd baked potatoes in the ashes and put together a salad.

Unfortunately, she couldn't taste any of it.

She put food in her mouth, chewed it and swallowed because she had a child's welfare to consider. Nourishment was important.

So was conversation, but neither of them made any.

It wasn't that she didn't have things she ached to say. Silly things, like, *Did you ever notice that the wind sighs like a lover's lament when it blows through the grass?* or *What a beautiful table this is,* or—or *I'd love to trace that little indentation between your mouth and your chin with my finger…*

"…would you?"

Marissa blinked. At first, she thought she'd spoken aloud, but then she realized Cullen was talking about the glass he was holding out to her.

"Marissa? Would you like something to drink?"

She stared at the glass while her heartbeat returned to normal. Then she managed a polite smile.

"Thank you, but I can't have any alcohol. The baby—"

"It's flavored mineral water." He gave her a quick smile. "Strawberry. I think I gave Peggy Denton a shock when I asked her to buy some and put it in the refrigerator."

Her fingers closed around the stem of the glass. "Peggy Denton?"

"Peggy and her husband, Tom, keep track of things here for me. I try to get up at least a couple of times a month but it's good to know somebody's keeping an eye on the place."

"Oh." *Come on, Marissa. You can do better than "oh."*

"Yes. I'm sure it must be a worry to have a second home."

"It's a joy," Cullen said. "Having this place, I mean. And I don't think of it as my second home, I think of it as my only home. The Boston place is just—what's the phrase? It's just where I hang my hat."

"Well, I can understand that. This place is lovely."

"I'm glad you like it."

"I'm sure everyone who sees it likes it."

She looked up, met his gaze and blushed. What a pathetic ploy! And for what reason? Why should it matter to her if he'd brought a hundred women to his house?

"No one's seen it," he said quietly. "Just you."

"I don't understand."

"Yeah. You do." His eyes seemed to burn through her. "You were trying to figure out how many other women I've brought here."

"You flatter yourself," she said coolly. "Why would I care?"

"I don't know." His voice was low, almost a whisper. "I've got some ideas, but only you have the answer."

"I really don't know what you mean. Who you've invited here isn't my—"

She gasped as he leaned over the table and caught her by the wrist.

"Don't you think it's time we stopped the subterfuge?"

Marissa pushed back her chair. She tried to rise, but he wouldn't let her. She could feel her heart racing in the hollow of her throat. What kind of admission was he trying to wring from her? Whatever it was, she knew better than to give it.

"Let go of me, Cullen."

Cullen got to his feet, tugged Marissa from her chair and pulled her into the heat and hardness of his body.

"We spent one night together," he said roughly. "That's all—but I never forgot it."

"Did you hear what I said?" She slammed her hands against his shoulders. "Let go!"

"Answers first, damn you! Tell me that night didn't mean a thing to you and I'll turn around and give your precious solitude back to you."

"It didn't."

"I don't believe you."

"Great! You say you want answers but what you really mean is that you want answers that suit you!"

"What I want is the truth—or don't you know what the truth is anymore?" His hands clasped her shoulders; his eyes burned into hers. "You drove me out of my head that night. I'd never felt that way with a woman before."

"Stop it!" Marissa slapped her hands over her ears. "I don't want to hear—"

Cullen grabbed her hands, brought them to his chest.

"I thought about you all the time. I dreamed about you. Do you know what it was like to find out that what happened between us hadn't meant a damned thing to you?"

"Stop it! Stop it!"

"How could you have trembled in my arms, cried out my name, taken me so deep inside you that I couldn't tell where I ended and you began, if it meant nothing?" Cullen tunneled his fingers into Marissa's hair, forced her to look at him. "Tell me, damn you, or—or—"

"Or what?"

Her whisper hung in the air. He looked into her silver eyes, at her trembling mouth and the telltale pulse pounding in her throat, and knew he could take her now, that he was right, her anger was only a cover for what she wanted.

Him.

She wanted him as much as he wanted her... But he wouldn't take her like this.

Not in rage. Not in denial of whatever was driving them both. His wife would come to him willingly. Open her arms to him. Sigh his name, as she had the night they'd conceived their child, or this would only be sex...

And he—he wanted more than that.

Hell, what was happening to him? He felt as if he were standing on the brink of a precipice that waited to swallow him in darkness.

Cullen lifted his hands from her shoulders and stepped back.

"It's late," he said gruffly. "Go to bed."

"Cullen," Marissa murmured, tasting tears on her lips.

"Do us both a favor, okay?" He turned away, clasped the edge of the mantle with both hands and bowed his head. "Get out of here."

Marissa stared at the stranger who was her husband. Then she turned and fled.

CHAPTER TEN

AN IVORY swath of moonlight danced on a black sea. Stars glittered with cold brilliance against the night's ebony canopy and streamed through the skylight over Cullen's bed.

It was a view that had the power to make him see his home as a clipper ship sailing across a vast, wind-blown sea of marsh grass.

Tonight, for the first time since he'd added the skylight to the house, Cullen took no pleasure in it.

All he could think of was Marissa and the disaster that was their marriage.

He knew he should be exhausted from the long day and longer evening, but even though his body cried out for sleep, his mind wouldn't stop whirling.

Why had he brought her here?

Why had he thought it would change anything?

Most of all, why had he imagined he could make this marriage work?

Cullen rolled over on his belly and punched his pillow into shape.

He could tell by the angle of the moon that it was very late, the time that came in the deepest part of the night when small creatures scuttled about on the moors and the brush of the wind made the old house sigh.

He could hear the booming who-who-who-hooo of a hunting owl. The creak of a floorboard and the steady beat of the ocean's heart as it flung itself against the shore.

What he wanted to hear was the whisper of his wife's breath as she slept in his arms.

That was the reason he couldn't sleep. Each time he closed his eyes, he imagined how it would be to have her here, beside him. To feel her lying close against him.

But none of that would happen. Marissa lay in the next room, separated from him by far more than a wall. Was she awake? Was she waiting?

Cullen sat up and ran his hands through his hair.

If she was waiting, it was only to leave this place. To leave this marriage.

To leave him.

He snarled an oath, got to his feet and pulled on his jeans. What a hell of a mess he'd gotten himself into. Married to a woman who couldn't stand him, and for what? He should have listened to Sean. He should have given his child his name, his financial support, and if he'd wanted to carry things further, he could have been a long-distance father. Lots of men were and no, it wasn't a perfect way to raise a kid, but it could have worked.

Maybe it still could.

Cullen looked at the clock on the night table. It was almost three-thirty. The middle of the night, back in Boston. The start of the day for those whose lives were still governed by the sea on this dot of land off the coast of Massachusetts. The commercial fishing boats would be leaving the harbor soon, followed not long after by boats that took sport fishermen out to sea.

And he'd still be trapped here, in a house with a woman who despised him, wondering what in hell he was going to do with her.

With his life.

A chilly breeze fluttered the vertical blinds, blew over his bare skin. Cullen shuddered and closed the window. The house was cold, even though he'd made sure to turn up the heat because of Marissa.

Was she warm enough? Had she paid any attention at all when he'd knocked at her door and told her there were extra blankets in the closet?

Maybe he should knock on her door again. Ask her if she was okay. Maybe…

Maybe he was an idiot.

His wife wasn't a child. She could figure things out for herself. If she wanted another blanket, she'd find one. Just because they were separated by only a wall didn't mean he had to think about her constantly. Back in Boston, the master suite and the guest suite were on different levels of the town house, which meant she was never in his thoughts at night…

Who was he kidding? In Boston, he lay awake for hours, wondering what would happen if he went to her room, opened her door, went to her bed.

And because he knew what would happen, that Marissa would greet him with all the warmth of a princess greeting the ogre who held her captive, he always ended up standing under the merciless spray of an ice-cold shower.

What could be more pathetic than that?

This. What he was doing now. Pacing his room, lost in erotic fantasies and damning himself for bringing her here.

Enough.

Cullen dug a turtleneck sweater from a drawer, pulled it on, zipped up his jeans and stuck his feet into a pair of well-worn mocs. Once in the hallway, he went by Marissa's door without glancing at it, turned up the thermostat at the head of the stairs and then made his way down to the kitchen.

The icy breath of the old stone floor bit straight through his moccasins. He thought about going back upstairs for wool socks but he'd have to pass Marissa's room again and he didn't want to do that.

No special reason for it, just—just that he didn't want to take the chance on disturbing her.

Maybe a hot drink would chase away the chill.

There was just enough light in the kitchen for him to take down a heavy white mug and fill it with some of the coffee he'd brewed after dinner. He'd made herbal tea for Marissa but, of course, she'd refused to drink it.

Why would she want to drink his tea when she didn't want his baby?

No, he thought as he put the mug in the microwave oven, that wasn't true. She wanted the baby. She just didn't want to think of it as his.

Numbers flashed on the timer pad; Cullen opened the door before the buzzer could sound. He wrapped his hands around the mug of coffee, took a sip, felt its warmth slip through his blood.

He felt better already.

Sipping at the hot liquid, he walked slowly into the living room and stood by the window.

It would be dawn soon. The moon had set; the stars were getting dim. Clouds were rolling in over the ocean. Great. The day was probably going to be gray, raw and wet. Just right to match his mood.

If Marissa wasn't up by six, he'd knock on her door. No point in dragging things out. The sooner they left this place, the better.

Cullen started toward the stairs, thought about walking past that closed door again and turned back. There was no point in going to his room now. He might as well settle in down here and wait for daybreak.

He headed for the sunroom. It was his favorite room in the house.

He'd added it at the same time he'd added the skylight. Like the skylight, he'd thought long and hard before doing it. The house, severe of line and elegant in its simplicity, was almost 200 years old and had been built by a whaling captain in the days when whaling was a sad industry in these waters.

He hadn't wanted to spoil the lines of the house, but he had wanted to open it so it could look out on the sea and the sky. A crazy thought, maybe, though when he'd voiced it to an architect, the guy had looked at him, smiled and said yeah, he could see how that made sense.

It wasn't historically accurate to put a sunroom on a house like this but the architect had been careful with the design, making the room's proportions fit the house. The sunroom had a planked floor, glass walls and a glass roof. Cullen had furnished it simply. A small sofa, a couple of chairs, a coffee table, and the room's centerpiece, an antique telescope.

On a morning like this, he might be lucky enough to spot a whale breaching. That might improve his mood.

The door to the sunroom was closed, though he didn't recall shutting it. He turned the door knob, stepped inside…

And walked straight into his soft, sweet-smelling wife.

Marissa gave a thin scream. He danced back. The coffee, still hot as blazes from the microwave, sloshed onto his fingers.

Cullen said something a gentleman wasn't supposed to say, especially around a lady.

Marissa clutched what looked like his shirt around her. "Did you ever hear of knocking?"

"Did you ever hear of turning on a light?"

"What's that got to do with you scaring me out of my skin?"

"About as much as you giving me a third-degree burn. If you'd put a light on, I'd have seen you."

"If you weren't sneaking around in the dark, you'd have seen me." She paused. "How'd I burn you?"

"Coffee," Cullen said brusquely. "And I wasn't sneaking around in the…" He frowned. "Are you okay?"

"You mean, did I survive being run over by a truck?"

He sighed. "I didn't meant to scare you."

"And I didn't mean to burn you." Marissa paused. "Where?"

"Never mind. It's nothing."

She switched on a table lamp. She was wearing one of the shirts he'd left on the railing. She had it buttoned from top to bottom. The soft cotton bulged out gently over her belly and hung to mid-thigh.

How could a man's shirt on a pregnant woman's body look sexy?

God, she was beautiful.

"Where?" she demanded again.

Cullen blinked. "What?"

"Oh, for pity's sake! Where's the burn?"

Right here, he thought. Inside me.

"My fingers. But it's nothing."

Marissa grabbed his hand and examined it as carefully as a miner panning for gold.

"There's nothing there."

He nodded. "That's what I said."

"You said…" She huffed out a breath. "Fine. In that case, good—"

Cullen wove his fingers through hers as she started to brush past him. "Where are you going?"

"Upstairs. To bed. Where else would a person go in the middle of the night?"

"I don't know," he said lazily. "Maybe down to the sunroom, because she can't sleep." His hand tightened on hers. "Or because he can't sleep, either. Interesting, don't you think? That two people with insomnia should be prowling the house in the middle of the night?"

Color stole into Marissa's face. "I always have trouble falling asleep when I'm overtired."

"Hell." The smile that had begun angling across his lips disappeared. "Of course you're overtired. It's my fault."

"It has nothing to do with you."

"Sure it does. I'm the one dragged you all over Massachusetts today."

"There's nothing tiring about sitting in a car or a plane when someone else does all the work," she said stiffly.

"There is, if you're pregnant."

"I'm just tired, that's all. I—I didn't sleep very well last night."

"No. Me, either." Cullen's gaze narrowed on her face. "Your eyes are red."

"Are they?" She gave a little shrug and drew her hand free of his. "Well, as I said, I'm—"

"Tired. Yeah, I know, but…" His brows drew together. "Have you been crying?"

She jerked back, as if he were the one who'd burned her this time.

"Of course not! Why would I—"

"You were." He reached out a hand. She jerked back again but not quickly enough. His thumb brushed gently over her lashes and came away damp with what surely were tears. "Marissa. Are you sick?"

"I'm fine. I'd be even better if you'd let me get past you and—"

His hand closed on her shoulder. The sight of her swollen eyes frightened him. She hadn't wept, not once since their marriage. Angry tears, yes. But these weren't angry tears, they were tears of sorrow.

"Why were you crying?"

"I just told you, I wasn't."

"Don't lie to me," he said harshly. "You were, and I want to know the reason."

Their eyes met. She sank her teeth lightly into her bottom lip before tearing her gaze from his.

"I'm pregnant," she said coolly. "Pregnant women cry a lot."

"Over…?"

"Over nothing. Over everything." She turned away and gave a little laugh. "You want the truth? I heard an owl hoot. And a second later, I heard this terrible little cry…"

Her voice broke. Cullen sighed, clasped her shoulders and turned her toward him.

"The owl has to live," he said quietly.

Marissa nodded. "I know. I do, really. But—but I thought, what if it's that rabbit we saw this afternoon? One minute, so full of life. And the next—the next—"

"When I was a kid," he said cupping her face in his hands, "maybe eight or nine, I went fishing with my father. It was a big event, getting to spend the day with the old man. He was hardly ever home and when he was, he wasn't the kind of guy played much with his kids, so I don't know how I ended up with him that day. Maybe Sean and Keir were sick. Maybe the girls were off somewhere with Ma. Anyway, Pa took me fishing. And—"

"And," Marissa said, "you had a wonderful time."

The way she made the words sound told him she was hoping for a fairy-tale ending. He knew it was important to her, though he didn't know why, but there hadn't been many fairy-tale endings where he and his old man were concerned.

So he smiled, brushed his mouth over hers and realized, only after he'd done it, that he'd felt the sweet softening of her lips under his as he'd kissed her.

"We had a terrible time. Nothing I did came out right. He showed me how to bait my hook, and I still got it wrong. When I cast, I kept on snagging the line. I moved around in the boat when I should have kept still and kept still when I should have been moving."

Marissa's eyes filled. "That's so sad!"

"It's just the way it was, sweetheart." Cullen tucked a curl behind her ear. "But on the way home, my father suddenly pulled into a parking lot outside this store that sold the best ice cream in town. He bought me a strawberry cone—my favorite. A double dip, with sprinkles. I didn't even have to ask for the sprinkles. He just knew I wanted them."

"See?" She gave him a watery smile. "You had a good time after all."

Gently, he brushed his thumbs under her eyes and wiped away her tears. "Yeah. But I was too young to get the real message of that day. It didn't hit me until years later."

Marissa raised her eyebrows. "The real message?"

Cullen nodded. "Life's impossible to predict. Sometimes

what starts badly ends well.'' He lifted her face to his. ''Just as circumstances put me in that boat with my father, circumstance forced us into a marriage neither of us was ready for, but what happens next is what we make of it.'' He bent to her and kissed her again, felt her lips cling softly to his. ''Marissa? We can make this work, if we try.''

She stared up at him. ''I don't—I don't…'' Her voice broke. ''I wish things were different, Cullen. I wish—''

''We can make them different,'' he said, looking deep into her eyes. ''I know we can.''

She was crying openly now, the tears spilling down her cheeks, and his throat tightened. He didn't want to make her cry. He'd never wanted that. All he'd wanted, from the start, was to do the right thing…

The right thing, Cullen thought, and covered his wife's mouth with his.

He meant the kiss to be tender. An apology for making her cry. A promise that he would try to make their marriage work. But his name sighed from her lips to his, her body softened as he drew her close, and he was lost.

''Cullen,'' she whispered, and she lifted her hands, flattened her palms against his chest, opened her mouth to his.

She tasted like the first sweet drops of rain, pattering against the glass roof of the sunroom. Like the delicate flowers that bloomed on the moor grasses in summer. His heart began to race; his body hardened.

''Marissa,'' he said, his voice rough, the warning in it implicit.

She answered by rising on her toes and winding her arms around his neck.

Cullen groaned, angled his mouth over Marissa's and deepened the kiss.

''Yes,'' she whispered, and moved against him…and almost drove him to his knees.

There was no mistaking the message.

She wanted him, just as she'd wanted him that night. As he'd wanted her all these months.

Cullen pressed his lips to his wife's throat. Her head fell back as he touched the tip of his tongue to the hollow of it where her pulse matched the race of his.

One by one, he undid the buttons that went from collar to hem down the front of her shirt, his mouth following after his fingers as he kissed her throat, her collarbones, the elegant valley between her breasts.

When the final button was undone, he cradled her breasts in his hands, exulting in their new, luxuriant weight. He dipped his head, licked the aroused tips, drew first one and then the other into his mouth, loving their remembered taste and Marissa's soft moans of pleasure.

Cullen lifted his head, watched his wife's face as he feathered his fingertips over her nipples. Her eyes were dark, almost blind with rapture. Her lips were parted, her breathing swift and shallow.

"Do you like it when I do this?" he said thickly.

"Yes," she whispered, "oh, yes, yes, yes..."

Her soft admission sharpened the need that burned, hot and fierce, in his blood. He'd wanted Marissa the night they'd slept together, more than he'd ever wanted another woman, but not like this. Never like this. Desire pounded through him with each beat of his heart. For sex, yes. For possession of her body, yes. But for more, much more than that.

It was desire for Marissa that filled him. For her, for her alone.

He wanted to tell her that, but how could he speak when she was easing her hands under his sweater? When she was moving against him in an ancient rhythm that had not changed in thousands and thousands of years?

Cullen slid his hands down his wife's back, loving the silken glide of her skin against his callused palms. He cupped her bottom, lifted her, brought her tight against the heat and hardness of his erection.

"The baby," she whispered, and he felt a moment of terror.

"Am I hurting him?"

Marissa gave a throaty little laugh. "No. Oh, no. We can't hurt him this way. I only meant… My body's not the same, Cullen. I don't look like—like the woman you made love to that night."

No. She didn't. He already knew that. He'd tasted the ripe sweetness of her breasts, felt the roundness of her belly pressing against him.

"I know that," he said, and slowly drew the shirt from her shoulders. She tried to grab it, but it slid free of her hands and dropped to the floor.

"Cullen," she said with an embarrassed little laugh, lifting her arms and covering herself.

"I want to see you," he said softly.

He took Marissa's hands, brought them to his mouth, kissed the palms, gently eased them to her sides and looked at his wife. His beautiful wife.

His exquisite Marissa.

Her breasts were full and lush, the nipples dark as the sweetest cherries. Her belly was rounded, filled with the child they'd created together. And her face…her face was filled with desire. With joy.

With something it almost took his breath away to see.

"I—I gained weight," she said hesitantly.

He smiled. "I should hope so."

"I mean—I mean, I look—I look—"

"You look like my wife," Cullen said, as he swung her into his arms and carried her through the dark house and up the stairs to his bed.

CHAPTER ELEVEN

MARISSA clung to Cullen's neck, her face nestled in the hollow of his throat, as he carried her into his bedroom.

She was naked; he was still dressed. The rough textures of his clothes against her sensitive skin seemed to heighten her soft vulnerability, his hard masculinity. How could such a simple difference be so erotic?

He laid her down in the center of his bed and came down above her, his hands pressed to the mattress on either side of her body. He kissed her slowly, urging her to open to him, to let him taste her, to taste him in return.

And yes, oh, yes, Marissa returned those kisses. She loved the feel of his teeth sinking gently into her lower lip, the thrust of his tongue. On a soft moan, she reached up to draw him down to her.

Instead, he sat back, brought her hands to his lips, kissed the palms, sucked the tip of one index finger into the warmth of his mouth. Then, his eyes never leaving hers, Cullen pulled his sweater over his head and shucked off his jeans.

The room was lit with the pale luminescence of dawn. Marissa looked at the man who had been her lover for one night and who was now her husband.

He was beautiful, just as she'd remembered. How many nights had his image tormented her? His saint-and-sinner face, all hard planes and elegant angles. His shoulders, wide and taut with muscle. His powerful, lightly furred chest, tightly defined abdomen, narrow hips...

Her gaze skittered past his navel. A rush of heat surged

through her body, from her breasts to her loins. He was erect, fully aroused.

"Marissa," he whispered, and she raised her eyes to his and opened her arms.

Cullen came down beside his wife and kissed her, tunneling his fingers through her hair, pressing her back into the yielding softness of the big bed. She sighed against his mouth, said his name in a sweet whisper.

He cupped her breasts, kissed them, sucked on them. Moaning, she arched her back, lifting herself, and he accepted the offering, worshiping with hands and mouth this woman he had so long wanted. Gently, he ran his hand over the rounded contours of her belly, bent his head and pressed kisses over the taut skin, parted her thighs and cupped her hot, secret center. She cried out and he thought he'd go over the edge just from the sound of her voice, from the way she writhed beneath him, from the wetness of her.

God, she was so wet! For him. Only for him.

He kissed her deeply, stroked her deeply, and she gave a sharp, keening cry that tore through his heart.

"Marissa," he said thickly, and when he touched her this time, it was with his mouth.

She jumped at the first stroke of his tongue against her engorged flesh.

"No," she said, "Cullen..."

She reached down to stop him, but somehow, somehow her hands tangled in his hair and instead of pushing him away, she held him closer, held his mouth on her, and all at once she came apart, came against his kisses, his wild, wonderful kisses. Colors exploded behind her closed eyelids; a river of flame swept through her veins, and then Cullen moved up her body, entered her, filled her, slipped his hands beneath her and urged her on and on and on while she clung to his shoulders...

And when he cried out and spilled himself into her, Marissa echoed his cry and tumbled off the edge of the world, safe at long last in her husband's arms.

THEY slept, curled in a lover's embrace.

Cullen woke first, to the sound of rain, the pale light of morning, and to the wonder of his wife, her body tight against his as she lay sleeping in the curve of his arm.

Carefully, he eased onto his side, still holding her close. Marissa murmured in her sleep, shifted easily with him and he gathered her closer, loving the feel of her breasts against his chest, her belly against his belly.

He slid his hand down her back, stroking his fingers lightly over her skin, cupping one buttock and lifting her into him. She sighed, wound her arm around him as she slept.

A hand seemed to reach inside his chest and tighten around his heart.

My wife, he thought. His beautiful, brave, defiant, incredible wife.

God, he was so happy! He'd never felt so happy be—

Marissa jabbed him with her elbow.

"Hey," he whispered. "Sweetheart? Are you awa—"

Another jab. Sharper this time, but how could it be her elbow? She was lying with one arm wrapped him and the other wrapped around her pillow.

Jab. Jab, jab, jab…

Oh, man! Cullen's eyes widened. His wife wasn't poking him in the gut.

His son was.

Carefully, he drew away just enough so he could push down the blankets. Something—a tiny elbow, maybe, or a little knee—made a ripple in the smooth skin of Marissa's belly.

Holy Hannah.

A grin spread over Cullen's face. "Hey, pal," he said softly.

Another poke. A delicate undulation. Then nothing. Cullen waited, caught his lip between his teeth, finally laid his hand lightly over his wife's tummy. A second passed, and then he felt it. A wave of motion. A feathery brush against his palm.

His baby was moving within his wife's womb.

Cullen felt his throat constrict.

Before he met Marissa, he'd thought he owned the world. If Aladdin's lamp had suddenly appeared and he'd rubbed it and a genie burst from the spout and said, *Cullen O'Connell, you have one wish,* he'd have said, without even stopping to think, *Tell you what, Mr. Genie. I don't need a thing. I already have everything I could possibly want.*

How wrong he'd been.

These were the things a man needed. A child to love. A woman in his arms. A woman he—a woman he—

"Mmm."

Marissa was waking up. He watched as she opened her eyes and focused on his face. A slow, shy smile curved her lips. How could a smile make a man feel so good?

"Good morning," he said softly. She smiled again and he bent his head and kissed her.

"I didn't mean to wake you," he whispered against her mouth. He stroked her stomach. "But I was getting acquainted with our son."

She looked at where his hand lay. His gaze followed hers.

"He made the introduction," Cullen said, and grinned. "Kicked me. Hard."

Marissa gave a soft laugh. How lovely it was to wake up, safe and warm, in the circle of your husband's arm, and to have the added bonus of hearing him sound as pleased as if their unborn child had already scored his first goal.

"He's been doing a lot of that lately," she said, reaching up and brushing a dark strand of hair from Cullen's brow.

"It's okay? I mean, he's supposed to jump around like that?"

"Uh-huh."

"He's not hurting you?"

She grinned. "No."

"I mean, I know kids move. I felt Cassie's baby when—"

"Cassie. Your brother's wife, right?"

"Uh-huh. She's due any day now, but when I was visiting them a while ago, the baby was kicking and Cassie let me feel..." Cullen frowned. "Sweetheart," he said softly, "I'm sorry. It just really hit me that you don't know anything about my family except the little I've told you."

"And I told you, I understand." Her smile wobbled around the edges. "The thing is, that there's probably never a good time to tell them that you had to get married."

He looked at her as if she'd lost her mind. "I don't intend to tell them that," he said gruffly.

Marissa nodded. What else had she expected him to say? She didn't know how he could raise a child without his family learning about it but then, she didn't know his family. He'd made it sound as if his brothers and sisters were close, but maybe they weren't. Maybe you could have a family and never tell them anything about your life. Anything was possible.

The only certainty was that she'd been a fool to think last night had changed anything.

"Of course," she said, sitting up and swinging her legs to the floor. The shirt she'd worn last night lay on the floor near the doorway. Was there a way to get there without letting go of the blanket? She'd never felt more naked in her life.

"Marissa?"

"Yes," she said briskly.

"Where are you going?"

"To get dressed. Well, to take a shower. Then I'll get dressed. And make some coffee. Some breakfast. Some—"

Cullen reached for her and pulled her back against him. "I don't want breakfast." He nuzzled her hair aside, bit lightly at the nape of her neck. "The only thing I want is you."

"Cullen." She drew a steadying breath. "Last night was—it was very nice. But—"

"Very nice?" He gave a soft, sexy laugh as he turned her to him and framed her face with his hands. "Come on, sweetheart. You can do better than that."

"What do you expect me to say? It was…fun."

His mouth thinned. "Fun," he echoed. There was a dangerous edge to his voice.

"Yes. And you're right, having—having sex once in a while will probably make our relationship easier to—"

Cullen crushed her mouth beneath his. Marissa cried out, held back, tried not to let herself feel the kiss, but she couldn't. She wanted this. Her husband's arms. Her husband's kisses.

Her husband's love.

Tears rose in her eyes.

He would never love her. But she could love him, just as she had all these empty, lonely months. Love him, make love to him, take what she could and hold it hidden in her heart.

"Cullen," she whispered, winding her arms around his neck, and kissed him back.

Long moments later, he drew her head to his chest and gently stroked his hand down her spine.

"It was more than sex," he said quietly. "I—I care for you, Marissa."

Of course he did. She was carrying his baby. She'd seen the look on his face, after he'd felt his son move this morning. Oh, what she'd give to see such love in his eyes for her, too.

"And you—you care for me, too." His hand cupped the back of her head and he urged her face up until their eyes met. "You do, don't you?"

Marissa nodded. "Yes. You're—" *You're everything a*

woman dreams of. "You're a good man, Cullen O'Connell. What woman wouldn't care for you?"

A muscle danced in his jaw. If she'd made such an admission yesterday, it would have shocked him. Today, it left him feeling empty. He didn't want his wife to think of him as a good man. He wanted—he wanted—

Cullen cleared his throat.

"If we try, we can make this marriage work."

She nodded again. "Yes."

He kissed her, gently this time, brushing his lips lightly over hers, and then he smiled.

"Did I hear you say something about breakfast?"

"You did," she said, smiling back at him.

"I don't suppose…"

"What?"

"Ah, it's nothing."

"What's nothing?" She drew back and raised her eyebrows. "What were you going to say?"

"Well, I don't want to boast, but—"

"But?" she said, laughing.

"But, I make a damned fine omelet."

"Good." She grinned. "Because I have to warn you, O'Connell, I'm lousy in the kitchen."

His grin was sexy and unabashedly male. "Yeah, but you're terrific in bed."

"Compliments won't change a thing," she said primly, even as she smiled. "I'm still the world's worst cook."

"Ah." Cullen put a finger under her chin and lifted it. "But you're a great law student."

"Yes." Her smile dimmed. "Well, I used to be…"

"And you will be again. When we get back home, I'm going to introduce you to some people I know at Harvard Law."

Oh, what he'd give to see that light blaze in her eyes just for him!

"Really?"

He nodded. "Absolutely. Until then, we're going to need

some sustenance. Here's the deal. I'll do the eggs if you'll play student.''

Marissa wrinkled her nose. "What the heck are you talking about?"

Cullen grinned. "The best law students are logical and imaginative.''

"Yes, but—"

"They're good at reading stuff and figuring out what it means.''

Marissa rolled her eyes. "Honestly, Cullen—"

"But some things are just beyond a man's comprehension. Even if he's a lawyer. You understand?''

"No," she said, pushing gently against his chest and scowling at him, "I do not understand! What are you talking about?''

"Biscuits.''

"Biscuits?''

"Uh-huh. See, I came up here one weekend last winter when it was cold as the Arctic. Snow, ice… Anyway, Peggy—"

"The female half of the couple that watches this place for you…''

"Right. Peggy laid in some supplies, the way she usually does. And one of the things she included was a box of biscuit mix.''

"Be still, my heart," Marissa said, slapping both hands against her breast. "You make great omelets, and you also know how to bake?''

"I've never baked a thing in my life. And once I read those biscuit instructions…I knew I never would.'' Smiling, he laid his forehead against hers. "I figure maybe you'd like to give it a try.''

Marissa ran the tip of her tongue over her bottom lip. "Because you never could convince another woman to come here with you and read those directions?''

Cullen clasped her face and lifted it to his. "Because I never wanted to share this place with anyone until you,'' he said huskily. He kissed her, a slow, soul-stealing meeting of mouths that made her giddy with pleasure. "I guess you could say we gave this bed its test run last night."

That wonderful look he'd seen in her eyes a little while ago was there again. This time, he thought, this time, it was for him.

"That's lovely to know."

He gave her another of those grins that all but melted her bones.

"What do you say? I'll do the eggs, you'll do the biscuits. Deal?"

"Just as long as you understand the biscuits might turn out to be hockey pucks."

Cullen grinned and put a hand over her belly. "Hey, what have we got to lose? Get the kid used to the game early, like his old man."

Marissa laughed. "Now you're going to tell me you were a star on the ice."

"Well," he said, flashing another smile, "maybe not a star but I was damned good. Actually, my game was football. Sean was the one who was the hockey star."

"Your brother."

"Uh-huh. My kid brother. Keir's the oldest. And there are the girls, of course."

Keep smiling, Marissa told herself, even if you never lay eyes on these people.

"Of course," she said politely.

"Fallon. She's a model. Well, she was a model but she got married last year and... It's a long story."

"Yes," Marissa said, even more politely, "I'm sure it is."

"And there's Megan. And Briana. Meg's an accountant, but she's not like any accountant you've ever met. I mean, how many CPAs do you know who're into sky-diving?"

"Not many," Marissa said, working to hang on to her smile.

"And Bree." Cullen snorted. "I swear, there's not a

practical bone in her body. She's our Dr. Doolittle. You know, talks to the animals... Hell, they're a tough bunch to describe. You'll just have to figure them out for yourself when you meet them.''

"Yes," she said again, "I guess... When I meet them?"

"Keir, first. He and Cassie only live a hundred miles away. Less, really." He cocked his head. "I've got a great idea. How about paying them a visit when we leave here?"

"Well. Well, I—I—" Marissa hesitated. "You said—I thought you said you weren't going to tell them that—that you and I had to get married."

"And I won't." Cullen smoothed a tumble of jet-black curls back from his wife's cheeks. "We'll tell my family the truth, sweetheart," he said softly. "That we met months ago, that we wanted to be together but that—well, that life got in the way somehow and we didn't find each other again until a couple of weeks ago." He smiled as he stroked his thumb over her parted lips. "Is that all right with you?"

Marissa swallowed hard. "It's very all right with me."

"Great. In that case, we've got a lot to do. Breakfast. A drive to the harbor, so I can introduce you to the 38-foot lady in my life. We'll take her out for a cruise next time we're here."

"I don't know. I mean, I don't—"

"You'll love her," he said, waving away her objections, "once you get to know her."

"But not today."

"Nope. Like I said, we have stuff to do. Food. The harbor. Got to hit a few shops, so we can buy you some sexy clothes."

"Sexy?" Marissa laughed. "Clothes do not look sexy on pregnant ladies."

"They will, on my lady." Another kiss, this one long and sweet. "And then," Cullen said softly, "we'll pay a visit to Keir. How's that sound?"

Marissa stared at him. It sounded like a fairy tale come to life, but she knew better than to believe in fairy tales.

"Hell," Cullen said, "I'm an idiot. That's too much for you, isn't it? Here you are, probably exhausted, and I'm running off at the—"

Marissa lifted her face and pressed her mouth to his.

"I'm not the least bit tired," she whispered. "It all sounds wonderful."

"You sure? Because if you want to take it easy—"

"Cullen."

He could tell by her tone the discussion was over, but he knew how to get the last word.

"Change of plans," he said. "We'll spend a couple of days here."

"Honestly, I'm not—"

"I know. We'll still drive to the harbor, do some shopping." Gently, he eased her down against the pillows. "But Keir and Cassie can wait a couple of days. There are better things to do first."

Marissa laughed softly, looped her arms around his neck and kissed him.

"How about breakfast?" she said softly.

He cupped her breast, feathered his thumb over her nipple and she caught her breath.

"How about it?" he whispered thickly.

"It can…" Her voice broke. "It can wait, too."

He dipped his head and licked her flesh. "Your nipples are the color of roses."

"They're more sensitive than ever," she whispered back. "The baby—"

"Am I hurting you?"

"Oh, no. No! I love it when—yes. When you do that. When you—oh. Oh, Cullen…"

Marissa's breathless sighs were all the answers he needed, and when she reached for him, closed her hand around his rigid flesh, Cullen rolled onto his side, turned her to him and drew her leg over his hip.

"Look at me," he said hoarsely. "I want to see your face as you take me deep inside you…"

His words, his touch, the feel of him entering her, excited her almost beyond endurance. She cried out, kissed her husband's mouth, gave him complete possession of her body, her soul…

And showed him, the only way she dared, that what she was really giving him was her heart.

CHAPTER TWELVE

THEY awoke to a morning of bright blue skies and golden sun.

Indian Summer had come to Nantucket Island. Warm days. Cool nights filled with passion.

Marissa lost all her inhibitions in her husband's arms. Cullen was an incredible lover: romantic, giving, demanding. His lovemaking could be as dangerously wild as the sea, as sweetly tender as the wildflowers that bloomed on the moors. For the first time in her life, Marissa felt free...

Free, except for being unable to say the three simple words that were in her heart. If only she could say "I love you" to Cullen.

Still, she was blissfully happy.

They strolled the beaches, all but deserted this time of year. He teased her about the shells and bits of sea glass she picked up, but he was the one who tucked them into his pockets and carried them home for her.

They drove to the harbor and the slip where his boat was docked. Marissa took one look at the sleek vessel, another at the look in her husband's face, and changed her mind about not liking the ocean and sailboats.

"Can we take her out?" she asked.

Cullen hugged her, said he loved knowing that was what she wanted but now that he thought about it, he'd rather wait until after the baby was born.

"It'll be easier for you then, sweetheart," he said, and she smiled and said yes, it probably would, and reminded herself that it would be silly to weep with joy just because he'd mentioned the future. He'd done it before, but only in terms of their child. This was different. She knew it was a little thing, but it made her happy.

Everything made her happy.

The little restaurant he took her to, where the captain greeted him by name.

"This is my wife," Cullen said.

The man kissed her hand, beamed at the sight of her belly and offered her a single, perfect red rose after seating them at a table.

Another first, she thought, almost dizzy with pleasure. Cullen hadn't introduced her to anyone before. *This is my wife,* Marissa kept thinking, *this is my wife...*

Were there any more beautiful words in the English language?

They strolled the cobblestones on Main Street, peering into shop windows. Cullen bought her clothes, soft-as-silk cotton drawstring trousers and loose, gauzy tops, more of them than she could ever wear. He bought her handmade sandals because she admired them and gold earrings for the same reason. She learned not to say a thing was pretty in hopes it would keep him from buying it for her, but that didn't work because he bought things for her, anyway.

"I don't need all this," she said, a little breathlessly as the bags and boxes piled up in his car, and Cullen grinned and kissed her and said needing the stuff had nothing to do with wanting her to have it.

They bought an elegant picnic lunch and ate it at Brant Point, watching the boats round the point in a gentle wind. At Jetties Beach, they munched on hot dogs and potato chips while they watched the windsurfers skitter across the water. Because she couldn't drink wine while she was pregnant, they toasted the spectacular sunset at Madaket with ginger ale in champagne flutes.

And when they returned to Cullen's house each evening, he undressed her slowly, lovingly, and made love to her until she wept quiet tears of joy.

Oh, yes, she was happy. So happy it terrified her.

Could it last? The question plagued her in the middle of the night and when Cullen awoke and found her standing at the window, staring blindly out over the sea, she told him she was up because her back ached instead of telling the truth, that it was her heart that was aching.

"Let me help you, sweetheart," he said, and he carried her to bed, turned her on her side, gently rubbed the ache away until his hands turned a little harder, until his mouth replaced his hands, until she could think of nothing but how much she loved him.

One morning, at breakfast, she asked him about the brother he'd mentioned visiting. She phrased the question with care—she didn't want to pry if he didn't want her to—but Cullen sat back, smiled and started talking about all his family.

He told her stories about his brothers and sisters that made her laugh, but she sensed the loneliness of his early years when his father dragged them all from town to town in pursuit of a dream.

"I must be boring you with all this," he finally said.

Impulsively, she took his hand, brought it to her lips and kissed his knuckles.

"How could I be bored," she said softly, "learning these things about the man I married?"

He gave her a look she couldn't decipher and she wished she could take back the words, because she feared what he might have heard in them. So she turned it into something simpler and said she was always interested in the details of people's lives and he gave her another look and said that wasn't very lawyer-like. They both laughed and the moment passed.

In the end, lying in his arms late one night, soothed by the sigh of the wind and the heartbeat of the sea, she told him about herself. The father she'd never known. The mother she'd never understood. The emptiness of growing up on the fringes of polite society and the first small victory when she'd passed the entrance exam for the honors high school her mother had said would never accept her.

Cullen was so quiet that she thought he'd fallen asleep. Or, rather, that she'd put him to sleep with her babbling. While she lay there wondering what on earth had made her tell him all that stuff, he suddenly rolled above her and kissed her until her mouth felt sweetly swollen.

"You're wonderful," he said softly. "Wonderful. And I—and I—"

She waited, heart pounding.

"And you?" she whispered finally, framing his face with her hands.

She saw his Adam's apple move up and down as he swallowed. "And I," he finally said, "hate to leave here tomorrow...but we have to, sweetheart. I wish we could stay longer, but I have a court appearance coming up."

Why did she feel like weeping? "Of course," she said brightly. "I understand."

Cullen kissed her again. "We'll stay longer next time."

"Next time," she repeated, but somehow, even as he began to make love to her, she found herself wondering if there would be a next time, or if these few days were all they'd ever know of happiness.

They flew to back to Hyannis the next morning, picked up Cullen's car and set off for Keir's home in Connecticut. And as the miles flew past, Marissa kept hearing her mother's voice whispering slyly in her ear.

Nothing lasts. Get that through your head, Mari. Nothing ever lasts, especially if you're stupid enough to hope it will.

BY THE time they crossed the Massachusetts border, Cullen was a wreck.

Marissa had come up with a dozen reasons for changing plans and heading to Boston, so he knew she was nervous about this visit, too.

Yeah, but no way could she be as nervous as he was.

Hartford, 60 miles.

The sign flashed by before he could really process it. If Hartford was sixty miles away, how far was Keir's vineyard? Ten miles? Twenty? Why in hell hadn't he paid more attention to the details the times he'd been to Deer Run? Why hadn't he noted where it was by comparison to a city like Hartford?

Why would he have bothered? Who gave a damn about things like that?

He sure as hell didn't.

The only reason it mattered now was so he could figure out how long he had before he parked in the driveway at his brother's place, stepped out of the car and said, *Hello, Keir, and man, have I got a surprise for you!*

He glanced at Marissa, seated beside him, back straight, eyes pinned to the road ahead, hands folded tightly in her lap... Except, she didn't really have a lap anymore. She had a belly. A baby belly. A belly bursting with baby.

I'm punch-drunk, he thought, and snorted. Marissa looked at him.

"Did you say something?"

Cullen shook his head. "No. I'm just..." He drew a breath, huffed it out. "We'll be at Deer Run soon."

She looked at him, then at the road.

"You'll like Keir. Well, maybe not right away. He can be... But you'll love Cassie. She's terrific."

Marissa nodded. After a couple of minutes, she cleared her throat. "Cullen? Are you sure you don't want to phone your brother again?"

"I phoned him already."

"Yes, but you told him you were coming to see him and that—and that you had a surprise. I mean, it's your family and you know best, but—"

"I know what I'm doing."

She looked at Cullen. Her husband sounded positive, but he looked like a man on his way to a dentist who didn't believe in anesthesia.

"Suppose I stay in the car? So they don't see that I'm pregnant. Not right away."

"Now, there's a great idea. We drive up, Keir and Cassie come outside, I introduce you and then I tell them you're going to stay in the car while I go inside. 'No,' I'll say, 'that's okay. Marissa likes cars better than houses. We'll have supper, sit around, whatever, and after you guys are tucked in bed, I'll sneak her in.'"

She looked at him and made a sound that was almost a laugh. "All right, that wouldn't work."

"No," he said calmly. "It wouldn't."

"Then—then how about this? We go inside, we talk for a while, sort of work our way around to the fact that we're—that we're married."

"Uh-huh. And do we get to that bit of information before or after they notice you're pregnant?"

Marissa glanced down at her stomach. "I guess they'll see that right away."

Cullen figured it was his turn to laugh, but he couldn't. How come going to visit Keir had seemed like such a fine idea right up until the second they got in the car and he pointed it west?

"Yes," he said, "they will. And unless my brother's taken a bottle of stupid pills lately, he's going to figure out, real fast, that there's got to be a reason I'm paying him a visit with a pregnant woman in tow."

"I'm not exactly 'in tow,'" Marissa said coolly.

"It's just a figure of speech."

"It's *your* figure of speech, just like the idea of this unannounced visit is *your* idea." She folded her arms. Maybe her hands wouldn't shake so much if she did. Maybe she wouldn't be so terrified if she got just a little bit angry. "Frankly, I think you should have handled this differently."

"Like how?"

"I don't know. Write him a letter."

"Excellent plan," Cullen said sarcastically. "*"Dear*

Keir, How're the grapes doing this year? How's Cass? Oh, by the way, I've got a wife and she'll be giving birth to my son in four months.'"

His son. Were they back to that?

"How about re-writing that letter?" Marissa said, her voice trembling. *"'Dear Keir, Guess what? I made this huge mistake and now I'm paying for—'"*

Cullen put out his arm as if to make sure her seat belt held, then made a hard right, pulled onto the narrow shoulder of the road and turned to Marissa.

"Did I say I made a mistake?"

"You didn't have to say it."

"If I want to tell you I made a mistake, I'll tell it to you. You got that, counselor?"

Marissa looked away from him. She wanted to make a mocking response but if she said anything at all, she was afraid she'd start to cry.

"Marissa? You understand?"

"Yes," she said, and then, to her chagrin, she burst into tears.

Cullen cursed, hauled her into his arms and held her tight.

"Don't cry," he said roughly, pressing kisses into her hair. "God, I'm sorry, sweetheart. I'm so sorry." Gently, he swept the hair back from her temples. "I told myself this would be easy and the truth is, it won't be. But we'll get through it. Okay?"

She nodded. Her nose was running, her eyes were tearing, she looked like a whale and she was going to meet the man her husband described as his tough-minded, some-times-difficult-to-deal-with big brother.

"We'll get through it."

Marissa's voice wobbled, but the proud lift of her chin almost killed him. Cullen pulled a handkerchief from his pocket.

"We will," he said firmly, drying her eyes. "Every-thing's going to be just fine." He brought the hankie to her nose. "Blow." She did, noisily, and he smiled at her. "Keir's a good guy. He'll be surprised but he'll get past it. You all right now?"

"Yes," she lied, "I'm fine."

"Good." Cullen dropped a quick kiss on her mouth and drove back onto the road. "Because I just recognized where we are. We'll be there in ten minutes."

Marissa was quiet as he made the turn onto the long drive that led to Deer Run. It was a good thing, too, because he couldn't have responded to anything she might have said, not with his stomach in his throat.

Whatever had possessed him to do this? She was right. He should have phoned or written or sent a message by smoke signal. Anything but just turning up cold to break his news.

It was only that yesterday, all the yesterdays since they'd reached Nantucket, showing up on Keir's doorstep had seemed the best way to tell his brother that he was married, that his wife was pregnant, that it was okay because he was happy.

That he'd married Marissa because it was the right thing to do and now—now, he was crazily, insanely, head-over-heels, forever-after in love with his own wife.

Holy hell!

He was in love with his wife.

How could that have happened? When? Why? Forget that. "Why" was a dumb question. Why did a man fall in love with one particular woman? Because he did, that was all. Because she was special. Beautiful. Brilliant. Tough. Gentle. Independent. And God, he loved her, he'd probably loved her since the night he'd first made love to her.

"Cullen?"

He had to tell her. But when? Not now, with the stone mansion at Deer Run looming ahead. When *did* a man tell his wife he'd fallen in love with her?

"Cullen?"

Marriage was one thing. Love was something else. And

he wasn't going to open himself up to her, pour out his heart unless he was a thousand percent sure she felt the same way.

"Cullen!"

He swung toward her. To hell with waiting. With being cautious. "Marissa," he said urgently, "I have to tell you something…"

"Look," she whispered, pointing straight ahead.

Keir was maybe half a dozen feet away, standing at the foot of the stone steps that led to his front door.

"Cullen," he called, his face creased in a big grin.

By the time Cullen stepped from the car, went around to the passenger side and held out his hand to Marissa, Keir's grin had changed to a puzzled smile. And when they walked toward him and Cullen said, quietly and carefully, "Keir, this is Marissa. My wife," Keir wasn't smiling at all.

"MORE salad?" Cassie said briskly, holding the earthenware bowl in her hands like a temple offering as she looked around the dining room table.

Keir and Cullen shook their heads. Marissa didn't even look up from the plate of untouched food in front of her.

"Well," Cassie said, even more briskly, "in that case, it's time for dessert. French apple pie. Sounds good, don't you think? I made it myself, too. I found the recipe in a magazine a few days ago and then I saw all these yummy new Granny Smiths at the farm stand up the road, so—so I'll just clear the table."

Marissa lurched to her feet. "I'll help."

"Oh. Oh, no, that's okay. I mean, you're probably tired. I mean, you're—"

The women's eyes met. "Pregnant," Marissa said flatly.

"Pregnant," Cassie repeated. "Just like me."

Keir looked up. *Not* just like you, his cold expression said.

"Fine," Cassie said quickly. "You can help me clear.

Matter of fact, you can help me put up the coffee. High-test for the guys, decaf for us because—''

''Because we're pregnant,'' Marissa said, her tone defiant.

Keir looked at Marissa again and she returned the look in kind. Did he really think he was going to intimidate her? There wasn't a thing anyone in this house could say would hurt her…

Except what Cullen had started to say just as they got here, what he'd tried to say again when they had a minute alone.

What he would say, once the evening was over.

Marissa snatched up her plate, went around the table and collected the others. Nobody had eaten. Nobody had attempted conversation. Keir hadn't said three words to her. He didn't have to. Those telling looks said it all.

And Cullen… Cullen looked like a living, breathing example of the old saying about being between a rock and a hard place.

Just for a moment, her heart softened.

He was trying his best, she had to admit. He'd held her hand all through the first awful minutes of their meeting with his big brother, slipped his arm around her as they climbed the steps to the front door of the stone mansion, rubbed his hand up and down her spine when Cassie came out of the kitchen, looking happy, hugely pregnant…

And shocked at the sight of her brother-in-law with a pregnant woman he introduced as his wife.

Alone in the room Cassie had shown them to, Cullen had taken her hands. Oh, if only he'd drawn her into his arms!

''I'm so sorry,'' he'd said. ''So sorry, Marissa.''

She'd nodded, not trusting herself to speak.

''I did this all wrong,'' he'd said, sounding fierce and angry. ''Damn it, I got it wrong from the beginning.''

Yes, he had. From the beginning. She'd known it. If only she'd been able to make him see it.

''But I'll make it right. I swear it. It's just not going to be the way we thought.'' He'd gotten this terribly serious expression on his face and said that he had something to tell her later.

And she'd nodded again because she knew what it was.

Their marriage was a disaster, never mind the last few wonderful days on the island. Sex was sex and responsibility was responsibility, but that didn't mean he'd had to marry her.

No question but Cullen knew that now. He'd made love to her, laughed with her, and maybe those things were okay, but he should never have married her. She was wearing the expensive clothes he'd bought her, the sandals, the gold earrings, but none of that changed the bottom line.

She didn't belong here, and her husband knew it.

She didn't fit in. Standing at the foot of the steps, looking up at his brother's cold face, the stone walls of his home rising behind him, she'd finally faced the truth.

These people were rich. They had Position and Power with capital Ps.

She was a Perez. A Mex. A *Chicano*. She had nothing. No position, no power, just a father she'd never known and a mother whose hobby had been bars and men.

She had no business in a setting like this or in a family like this. And Cullen had finally realized it.

''Marissa?''

She blinked. Cassie was standing in the doorway, a little smile on her lips.

''Did you want to bring those dishes into the kitchen?'' she said softly.

Marissa nodded. She felt Cullen's hand brush hers but she didn't look at him, she just kept putting one foot in front of the other until she was safely in the next room. Cassie gave her a pitying look. Damn it, the last thing she needed was pity, especially from an ivory-tower princess.

''Oh, Marissa,'' Cassie said, ''I'm so sorry...''

''Don't be ridiculous. There's nothing to be sorry for.''

"There is. My husband's behavior… He's just, well, surprised, that's all. Once he's had time to think—"

"Frankly, I don't give a damn what he thinks, now or later. I don't give a damn what you think, either." Marissa dumped the dishes in the sink and turned on the water. "As far as I'm concerned—as far as I'm concerned—"

She burst into tears.

"Oh, honey!" Cassie turned off the water and led her to a chair at the kitchen table. "Here." She yanked a wad of tissues from her apron pocket. Something metallic clinked against the tile floor and she bent and retrieved it. "There it is," she said. "I wondered what I'd done with the key to the SUV." Marissa hiccuped and Cassie tossed the key on the table and handed over the tissues. "You cry all you want while I go tell that dumb husband of mine—"

"No!" Marissa grabbed Cassie's hand. "Please don't. Cullen'll come in, he'll see me crying…"

"Why do you think I carry around those tissues?" Cassie said with a little smile. "Pregnant women cry all the time."

"Not like this." Marissa wiped her eyes. "I don't want him to know I'm upset."

"He knows already. He's upset, too. Heaven only knows what he's saying to Keir right now."

"I know what he's saying," Marissa said. "That he finally figured out our marriage was a huge mistake and that he's going to end it as soon as we get back to Boston."

"Oh, honey, no!" Cassie sat in the chair across from Marissa and reached for her hand. "He's crazy about you. Anyone can see that."

Marissa gave a watery laugh. "You mean, he's crazy to have married me. *That's* what anyone can see—especially your husband."

"Listen to me, Marissa. I love Keir dearly, but this is one of those times when he's being a pigheaded idiot."

"Cullen and I are wrong for each other, Cassie. It's sweet of you to try and make me think otherwise, but—"

"Keir's just surprised, that's all. He's very protective of

his brothers. He'll come around once he realizes how much Cullen loves you.''

"Cullen doesn't love me," Marissa said fiercely. "He only married me because I'm pregnant."

"Marissa. Honey, a man doesn't have to marry a woman because she's carrying his baby."

"Cullen was determined to do the right thing."

"Well, of course. He's an O'Connell." Cassie smiled and squeezed Marissa's hand. "What I meant was, he could have acknowledged your baby as his, provided for his support, for your support. He didn't have to take you as his wife. The fact that he did means—"

"It means he got carried away with doing the right thing."

"It means you matter to him."

"I don't."

"Marissa—"

"We only spent one night together!"

Cassie blinked. "Well, okay. I mean, it's unusual, sure, but some women get pregnant really fast and—"

"You don't understand. We only knew each other that one night." Marissa's face colored but she kept her eyes on Cassie's. "I met him," she said steadily, "slept with him, and never saw him again until I was almost four months pregnant. When he found out, he said we had to get married. And now—now, we both know it was a mistake. I know that's hard for you to understand. It must have been so different for you and Keir…"

Cassie laughed.

"It was different, all right. I despised him. He disliked me. The only thing we had in common was this overwhelming urge to climb into the sack together."

Marissa's eyes widened. "Are you serious?"

Cassie sighed, patted Marissa's hand and sat back in her chair.

"I'll tell you the entire story someday. For now, trust

me when I tell you that I wouldn't have bet ten cents we'd have fallen in love with each other.''

"Really?"

"Really. Hey, Mr. Keir O'Connell, entrepreneur, and Ms. Cassandra Bercovic, ex-stripper? Don't look like that, honey. It's the truth. I used to strip for a living.''

"That didn't bother Keir and his family?"

"Oh, it bothered Keir, but he got past it. As for his family…he loves them like crazy and so do I. They accepted me with open arms, but if they hadn't, that wouldn't have stopped him.'' Cassie leaned forward. "You hear what's happening in the next room? The raised voices? Assuming my husband's crazy enough to tell *your* husband he thinks this marriage was a mistake, I guarantee you that *your* husband is telling *my* husband what he can do with that opinion.''

Marissa felt her heart lift. "You think so?"

"I know so. That's how our men are. Independent. Tough. And fiercely loyal to the women they love and marry.''

"I told you, Cullen doesn't—"

"I think he does," Cassie said gently. "As for you…you're head over heels in love with him, aren't you?''

"Yes," Marissa whispered. "Yes, I am.''

Cassie patted her hand again, cocked her head and smiled. "The yelling's stopped.''

"Is that good?"

"Well, I haven't heard anybody bounce off the walls so yeah, it probably is. They've gotten past the shouting and now they're talking. Or waiting for us, so that Keir can apologize.'' She pushed back her chair. "What do you say? Shall we join our men?''

Our men. Marissa's face lit as she rose to her feet. "I'd like that.''

Together, the women walked into the pantry and toward the closed door to the dining room. Marissa touched

Cassie's shoulder just as Cassie cracked the door open. She needed one last minute to compose herself...

"...believe you did such a dumb thing," she heard Keir say.

Cullen's sigh carried the length of the room. "I know. It was worse than dumb."

Cassie swung toward Marissa, lips parted, but Marissa held up her hand. Cassie sighed, shook her head and stepped back so that it was Marissa who stood with her ear to the door.

"You're an attorney. You're supposed to know better than to get yourself into a mess like this."

"Look, spare me the lecture, okay?" Cullen's chair scraped as he pushed it back from the table. "I just admitted, getting married like that wasn't smart."

"I hope you left yourself some kind of out."

"Of course I did. I drew up a contract, added a clause that said the marriage was reviewable every two years."

"And?"

"And, tonight I'm going to tell her that the clause, the whole damned contract, is meaningless. I don't need two more years to know what I have to do."

"Now you're talking sense," Keir said.

Cullen added something, but Marissa had stopped listening. Eyes brimming with tears, she pushed past Cassie and ran into the kitchen.

"Marissa," Cassie said, "wait..."

But this was Cassie's ninth month. She was big as a house. Worse, she was clumsy. That was how she felt, anyway, as she waddled to the kitchen and wove through the chairs they'd left standing away from the table.

By the time she reached the back door, Marissa and the car key that had been lying on the table were gone.

CHAPTER THIRTEEN

CULLEN stared at Cassie as if she were speaking another language.

"Marissa did what?"

"She took off. How many times must I say it? Your wife's gone."

"Gone where? How?"

"I don't know where. And I already told you how. She took my key to our SUV."

Cullen shot to his feet. All at once, the message was getting through. It hadn't, at first, because it was so preposterous. Your wife took a stack of dishes into the kitchen, your sister-in-law ran in fifteen minutes later and said...

"My wife ran away?"

"Thank you, God," Cassie said dramatically, lifting her eyes to the ceiling. "Yes, you big jerk. She ran away."

The color drained from Cullen's face. "What happened?" he demanded. "Why'd she run?"

"She ran," Cassie said, her tone caustic as she thought back to a similar night in this very same house, "because the O'Connell brothers have the habit of saying things that sound bad within earshot of their women. You idiots sit here talking about what a mistake it was for Cullen to marry Marissa, how he's going to tell her tonight that the marriage is over—"

"What?"

"Oh, don't look so innocent, Cullen O'Connell! I heard you. More to the point, Marissa heard you. All that bull about how you built yourself a little exit clause into a marriage agreement, how you know now that marrying her was a mistake, how you have to tell her you want out…''

"That's what Marissa thinks I said?" Cullen said numbly.

"That's what she heard. So did I." Cassie's eyes shot sparks. "To think I was in there, defending you. Telling her not to cry, when all the time… She's crazy about you, Cullen. Are you blind? Couldn't you tell?"

Cullen got a strange look on his face. "She said that? That she's crazy about me?"

"What is it with you men? Stupid, as well as blind!" Cassie glared from her husband to her brother-in-law. "She's a wonderful woman. Are you incapable of seeing that?"

He'd been incapable of seeing a lot of things, Cullen thought. And now, his wife—his pregnant wife—was out there, in the dark, on a road she didn't know.

Cullen ran for the door. Keir went after him.

"Cull? Cull, wait. I'll go with you."

The door slammed. Cassie put her hand on her husband's shoulder and he turned toward her.

"He'll need help…"

Cassie shook her head. "He won't."

"Yeah, but—"

"He'll catch up to her and when he does, if he's anything like you, he'll do just fine." She smiled as she slid her hands up her husband's chest. "It may take him a while, but he'll convince her that he loves her. You convinced me, remember?"

Keir smiled back at his wife. He put his arms around her and linked his hands at the base of her spine.

"You're a devious witch."

"Uh-huh. And it's only one of the things you love about me."

He kissed her. Sighing, she leaned back in his embrace. "You were awful to Marissa."

"Yeah. Well, I thought she'd scammed him."

"He should have punched you out." Cassie grinned. "Of course, if he'd done that, I'd have had to slug him with a skillet, but he should have done it, anyway."

"He came close, after you and Marissa left the room. He chewed me out, said the only reason he hadn't done it sooner was because the two of you are pregnant, and he didn't want to upset you by taking me apart, limb by limb."

"Did you mean it when you told him he'd been dumb to marry Marissa?"

Keir shook his head. "You heard the tail end of the conversation. I started to give him hell. I said it was ridiculous to marry a woman he hardly knew, that he should have come to me for advice." He tilted Cassie's chin up. "He told me to mind my own business."

Cassie smiled. "Smart brother-in-law I've got," she said softly.

"And then he told me he loved her, and I said, well, that was different. And he said he hadn't told her yet, that he'd written this unenforceable clause into an unenforceable contract and that he was going to tell her that the bit about reviewing their marriage every two years wasn't just impossible, it wasn't going to happen because—"

"Keir?"

"—because he was never going to give her up, and I said—"

"Keir!"

"Yes, darling. I know. But it'll be okay. She can't get very far before he overtakes her."

"No. It isn't that."

"What is it, then?" Keir brushed his mouth over his wife's. "You want me to apologize to Marissa? I will, of course, the minute they get back."

"It isn't that, either." Cassie said. "It's the baby."

"What about the baby?"

"He's coming."

"Well, sure, but we still have almost two weeks—"

Something hot and liquid gushed over his feet. Keir went rigid. ''Cass?''

''The baby's coming now,'' she said, with a look in her eyes he'd never seen before.

''Now?''

''Right now,'' Cassie whispered.

Keir swung his wife into his arms, dug the keys to his sports car from his pocket and headed for the front door.

''Wait! I need my suitcase.''

''The hell you do,'' Keir growled, heading out into the night.

CULLEN drove fast, faster than was smart considering the narrow road and dark night, but that was okay because Marissa was on this road, too.

If anything happened to her…

No. He wouldn't think that way. Nothing bad could happen. Not now. She loved him, Cassie said. God, he hoped she did, enough to forgive him for the monumental ass he'd been.

He should have hauled Keir out of his chair five minutes into the evening, told him to start treating Marissa right or he'd beat the crap out of him.

But how could he, with Cassie sitting there, looking as if she were going to give birth any minute?

He should have leaned across the table, taken Marissa's hand and said, so they'd all hear him, ''Marissa, I love you.''

But how could he, when she might have answered, ''So what?''

Cullen stepped down harder on the gas.

Except, she wouldn't have said that. If he hadn't been so thick-skulled, he'd have figured things out for himself. What she felt for him glittered in her eyes whenever she smiled at him. It infused each whisper each time they made love. Walking the beach holding hands, lying in his arms in front of the fire… If he hadn't been so afraid to figure out his own feelings, he'd have been able to read hers.

She loved him.

When he found her, he'd tell her he loved her every hour on the hour for the next fifty years. The next hundred years. If only she'd listen. If she'd believe him. If…

Red taillights winked in the darkness ahead.

"Marissa," Cullen said.

He stepped down harder on the gas, blinked his lights. Marissa speeded up. Was she crazy? The road got even narrower here. With trees standing sentinel on either side, there was no room for error.

He blinked his lights again. "Slow down," he muttered, "damn it, Marissa, slow down!"

She went faster. Hell! What now? If he kept pushing, she'd just increase her speed. He dropped back, even though it was the last thing he wanted to do.

The lights ahead vanished. Cullen's mouth went dry as he tried to come up with a reason. Was there a bad curve up there? Some kind of drop-off?

No. He remembered now. There was a curve—that was why he'd lost Marissa's taillights—but it was an easy one. And just past it was the shoulder where they'd stopped on the way to Deer Run.

The lights came into view again. Cullen checked for traffic, sent up a prayer to whatever gods might be in the vicinity, stepped on the gas, sped ahead and passed the SUV. When he saw the shoulder, he stood on the brakes, turned onto it, jumped from his car and stepped out into the road.

He'd left her plenty of time to see him and to stop. Not that he gave a damn about what might happen to him; he just didn't want her to have to brake hard, or do anything to endanger herself or their unborn baby.

He knew when she spotted him. The SUV slowed—but she wasn't going to stop. She was going to swerve around him.

"Marissa," Cullen shouted, "Marissa, sweetheart, I love you!"

She couldn't have heard him, not over the sound of the car...

"I love you," he said, and after what seemed forever, Marissa swung the wheel, pulled onto the shoulder of the road and turned off the engine.

Cullen couldn't hear anything but the thud of his heart. The night was as silent as it can only be on a narrow country road. He took a deep breath and started toward the SUV. When he reached it, he grasped the door handle.

It was locked.

"Marissa. Sweetheart, let me in."

She wasn't looking at him. She was staring straight ahead and he knew she'd have folded her arms if she could, but there wasn't that much space between her belly and the steering wheel.

"Marissa. I love you."

She didn't answer. Didn't so much as look at him. He could hear the faint tick-tick of the cooling engine over the beat of his heart. He thought about the way she'd been driving, too fast, too hard, and what might have happened to her.

This time, when he tried the handle and called her name, anger roughened his voice.

Anger, at least, was an emotion he could deal with.

"Damn it, Marissa, open this door!"

She swung toward him. "No!"

"Open it, or—"

A car came roaring down the road. Cullen looked up as Keir's Ferrari raced past, slowing just long enough for him to see Cassie give him a thumbs-up through the open window as Keir tapped the horn.

"Go for it," she yelled.

Cullen turned to Marissa. "You hear that?" he shouted. "Cassie knows I love you. Keir knows it, too. The only person who doesn't know the damned truth is—"

The door opened. "Stop shouting," his wife said crossly, but not crossly enough to hide the catch in her voice. "You'll wake everybody up."

"There's nobody here but the damned cows."

"You're making enough noise to scare them silly." She hesitated. "What's all this nonsense about you loving me?"

"What's all this nonsense about you *leaving* me?" Cullen said gruffly.

"It's not nonsense, it's the first intelligent thing I've done since you came shouldering your way into my life."

"You're not leaving me, Marissa."

"I already have."

Cullen clasped her shoulders. "I'm not letting you leave me!"

"Did I spoil your plans? I know you were going to be the one to say, 'Goodbye, it's been interesting, but I'm ready to admit I made a huge mistake, and—'"

"I love you."

"Well, that's too bad, O'Connell, because it's too late for that. Listen and listen good, because I'm only saying this once. I'm the one who made a huge mistake. A gigantic mistake. A humongous mis—"

Cullen pulled her into his arms and kissed her. She struggled, but not terribly hard, and she started to cry even as her mouth softened under his, and that was when he knew, without question, that Cassie was right.

His wife loved him.

He took her by the shoulders again and held her just a couple of inches away.

"You love me," he said.

"Don't be stupid!" Tears were streaming down her cheeks but when he tried to wipe them away, she jerked back. "Why would I love a man who just told his brother how he's going to get rid of me?"

"What I told him was that I was going to get rid of that ridiculous piece of pseudolegal paper I showed you when we got married."

"You made a mess of things, you said."

"I did. I shouldn't have forced this marriage on you."

"Damned right, you shouldn't. Every good lawyer knows the importance of consultation."

"What I mean is, I shouldn't have come at you as an attorney." His voice softened. "What I should have done is woo you with flowers, told you what was already in my heart—"

"You don't have a heart," Marissa said, but not very convincingly.

"Well, I admit, it took me a while to find it. But I have one, sweetheart, and it's filled with love for you."

"Ha!" Marissa said, but he could see the glitter in her eyes that he'd been stupid enough to ignore until now.

"I love you. And you love me. And I'm not letting you move from this spot until you admit it."

"In that case, O'Connell, you're in for a long wait," Marissa replied, and ruined her answer by throwing her arms around his neck and kissing him. "I love you with all my heart," she whispered against his lips. "And I always will."

Cullen felt a sweet sense of relief. Knowing his wife loved him was one thing. Hearing her say the words was another.

"I should have told you."

She smiled. "Yes," she said gently, "you should have."

"Yeah." His voice roughened. "So I'll just have to tell you I love you morning, noon and night for the next hundred years, to make up for it."

Marissa leaned back in Cullen's arms and smiled. "Only three times a day for a hundred years? Doesn't sound like an appropriate damage award to me, counselor."

Cullen grinned. "You're a tough negotiator."

"I try," Marissa said sweetly.

He stroked his hand over her belly. "You hear that, pal? Your mom's going to be one heck of a fine attorney. Maybe she'll even agree to come on board at my firm."

Marissa laughed softly. "Is that a bribe?"

"Maybe," Cullen said, his smile fading and turning slow and hot and filled with promise. "On the other hand, I can think of some very creative forms of bribery to try, once I get you back to our room at Deer Run and into bed."

Her answering kiss took his breath away.

"If it's really, really creative," she whispered, "I might just be tempted."

Cullen helped Marissa into the SUV, got behind the wheel and started the engine.

"What about your Porsche?"

"It'll wait till morning." He reached for her hand, lifted it to his mouth and kissed her palm. "Making love to my wife won't."

Marissa thought about telling him that he was doing it all over again, making decisions that involved her without consulting her first…

But a smart lawyer knew that if the opposition came up with a plan you liked, the thing to do was smile and accept it.

THEY took their vows again, The Right Way.

Marissa Perez became Marissa Perez O'Connell on a clear-as-crystal late winter day in the glass-enclosed sunroom of their home on Nantucket Island. She wore a long, lovely white wedding gown; Cullen wore a tux, but their newborn son was the star attraction.

He was perfect. Ten fingers, ten toes, a shock of dark hair, and it seemed as if his eyes were going to be the same gray shade as his mother's.

In other words, he was beautiful.

So was Cullen, Marissa thought, and told him so, after the ceremony, right in front of his brothers, who were his best men, and they groaned and hooted so much that Cullen turned a bright pink.

"I'll get you for this," he whispered as he drew her close, and Marissa gave him a little smile that was so perfect and sexy that he just had to kiss her, right then and there.

His sisters and Cassie were Marissa's maids of honor. She'd come to love all the O'Connells, from her husband straight through to his warm and wonderful mother, Mary, and Mary's husband, Dan.

She told them that when Cullen was showing off his son and Briana, Fallon and Megan went into the bedroom with her to help get a snag out of her hem.

"I love you guys," Marissa said, and sniffed.

"For heaven's sake," Bree admonished, "don't cry or you'll ruin your makeup."

They all laughed, because they were all crying, and then Fallon got down to business, whipping a tiny tube of fast-drying glue from her beaded purse.

"I'll just put a drop on the hem," she said, kneeling in front of Marissa.

Bree grinned. "Ah, the things a woman learns during the years she's a supermodel."

Everybody laughed again. Seconds later, the little group trooped from the room. All but Megan, who hung back.

"You guys go on," she said. "I want to run a comb through my hair."

The door swung shut. Megan sighed and looked into the mirror.

Her new sister-in-law looked so happy. So did Cassie and Fallon, Cassie cuddling her baby, Fallon with her own pregnancy just starting to show, all of them gazing at their husbands with stars shining in their eyes.

Was something wrong with her? Was she the only woman on the planet who didn't want to get married? The only woman who didn't think she needed a man and babies to make her complete?

There was a light knock on the door.

"Yes?" Meg said, quickly brushing her hands over her eyes, which were, for some unaccountable reason, suddenly feeling prickly.

The door swung open. "Hey," Sean said, "you okay, sis?"

"I'm fine," she said, looking at him and smiling.

He held out his hand. "Got to stick together, kid, considering that there are only three of us O'Connells still sane enough to be single."

Megan laughed, took his hand and hurried along beside him to go and join the fun.

If you enjoyed what you just read,
then we've got an offer you can't resist!

Take 2 bestselling love stories FREE!

Plus get a FREE surprise gift!

The world's bestselling romance series.

HARLEQUIN®
Presents
Seduction and Passion Guaranteed!

OUTBACK KNIGHTS
Marriage is their mission!

From bad boys—to powerful,
passionate protectors!

Three tycoons from the Outback
rescue their brides-to-be....

Coming soon in Harlequin Presents:
Emma Darcy's exciting new trilogy

Meet Ric, Mitch and Johnny—once three Outback bad
boys, now rich and powerful men. But these sexy city
tycoons must return to the Outback to face a new
challenge: claiming their women as their brides!

**MAY 2004: THE OUTBACK MARRIAGE RANSOM #2391
JULY 2004: THE OUTBACK WEDDING TAKEOVER #2403
NOVEMBER 2004: THE OUTBACK BRIDAL RESCUE #2427**

**"Emma Darcy delivers a spicy love story...
a fiery conflict and a hot sensuality."
—*Romantic Times***

Available wherever Harlequin books are sold.

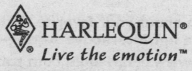

HARLEQUIN®
Live the emotion™

Visit us at www.eHarlequin.com

HPEDARCY

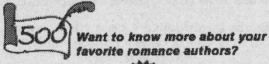

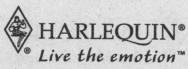

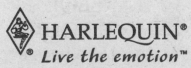

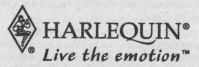

Coming Next Month

THE BEST HAS JUST GOTTEN BETTER!

#2391 THE OUTBACK MARRIAGE RANSOM Emma Darcy
At sixteen, Ric Donato wanted Lara Seymour—but they were
worlds apart. Years later he's a city tycoon, and now he can have
anything he wants.... Lara is living a glamorous life with another
man, but Ric is determined to have her—and he'll do whatever it
takes....

#2392 THE STEPHANIDES PREGNANCY Lynne Graham
Cristos Stephanides wanted Betsy Mitchell the moment he saw
her, shy and prim in her chauffeur's outfit, at the wheel of his limousine.... However, the Greek tycoon hadn't bargained on being
kidnapped—along with Betsy—and held captive on an Aegean
island!

#2393 A SICILIAN HUSBAND Kate Walker
When Terrie Hayden met Gio Cardella she knew that there was
something between them. Something that was worth risking
everything for. But the proud Sicilian didn't want to take that risk.
He had no idea what force kept dragging him back to her door....

#2394 THE DESERVING MISTRESS Carole Mortimer
May Calendar has spent her life looking after her sisters and running the family business—and she's determined not to let anyone
take it away from her! Especially not arrogant tycoon
Jude Marshall! But sexy, charming Jude is out to wine and dine
her—how can she resist...?

#2395 THE MILLIONAIRE'S MARRIAGE DEMAND
Sandra Field
Julie Renshaw is shocked when Travis Strathern makes an outra-
geous demand: marriage! She is very attracted to him—but
is she ready to marry for convenience? Travis always gets his own
way—but Julie makes it clear that their marriage must be based
on love as well as passion....

#2396 THE DESERT PRINCE'S MISTRESS Sharon Kendrick
Multimillionaire Darian Wildman made an instant decision about
beautiful Lara Black—he had to have her! Their mutual attraction
was scorching! Then Darian made a discovery that would change
both their lives. He was the illegitimate heir to a desert kingdom—
and a prince!